TRAILING REDEMPTION

KOREY J. KRUEGER

LifeRich
PUBLISHING

This is a work of fiction. All of the characters, names, incidents, organizations, and dialogue in this novel are either the products of the author's imagination or are used fictitiously.

LifeRich Publishing is a registered trademark of The Reader's Digest Association, Inc.

LifeRich Publishing books may be ordered through booksellers or by contacting:

LifeRich Publishing
1663 Liberty Drive
Bloomington, IN 47403
www.liferichpublishing.com
844-686-9607

ISBN: 978-1-4897-3620-8 (sc)
ISBN: 978-1-4897-3621-5 (hc)
ISBN: 978-1-4897-3619-2 (e)

Library of Congress Control Number: 2021910327

Print information available on the last page.

LifeRich Publishing rev. date: 05/19/2021

Contents

CHAPTER 1

SHOWER PARTY

Fully stretched out on the couch, with crumbs on his chest from recently eaten potato chips, Billy reached inside, only to find the bag was empty and would not provide or reveal another chip. As he stretched, the bag made strange noises, and crumbs fell to the floor. He was a pathetic sight, but he didn't care. He didn't think about how he looked or how ridiculous he may seem to anyone who would witness his weakened state.

Just then the front door was unlocked, and a small army of family members entered the living room. Billy's wife, Sarah, was the leader, both trying to pull her keys from the door and balance an armful of bags as one by one the others came through the entrance. As a group, they seemed out of breath and in a hurry. Sarah, more so than the children, was out of sorts and flustered. It seemed as if she could drop everything in her hands and still have over one hundred directions she could focus her attention. She was accustomed to taking care of everything. She had to take care of everything.

Billy was not one to take charge of anything, and he liked it that way. They all momentarily stopped, however, as a group to look at their patriarch, each developing their own expression of minor disapproval and pity.

They knew him well. He was not a complex man, or at least he wasn't while they knew him. They had grown accustomed to his malaise and melancholy. He took no passion in his work or in the family. Not one of them could provide insight into his hobbies or interests, as he had none. He avoided family, community, and church gatherings. Billy hated small talk and easily grew bored of the news of the day. His existence was limited and small, and his influence on his family and those around him was incomplete.

Billy rose slightly and slowly. He showed an almost disapproving look for their intrusion into his isolated world. He relished the moments of peace and quiet. Billy would rather nap after a day of work than do anything. They recognized his mild irritation, attitude, and emotion, as he had displayed it so many times before. Sarah organized the children into the kitchen and pantry. Billy could hear them rummaging through paper bags, putting away groceries and other items. Sarah was lucky they were such a helpful bunch. She reentered the living room and looked sternly at Billy.

"There is a party for you tonight, remember?" she asked, almost realizing she not only knew the answer to the question but also knew she had wasted time and energy on something he did not want anyway.

"Yes, I remember," he mumbled.

"Are you going to get ready? You have ruined that shirt, so you will need to change," Sarah said, showing her frustration. "Come on, people will be here soon!"

Billy looked down at his shirt, smiling devilishly, and whimsically chuckled. With reverence, he grabbed the bottom of the light blue shirt he had worn to work, pulled it outward to get a better look, and admired how the oil from the chip crumbs had penetrated the material. He was not an evil person, but the part of a person that would be considerate to the feelings and needs of others around him was broken. It was broken a long time ago. Billy had a chip on his shoulder.

"What's wrong with this shirt?" he asked jokingly.

"Get your ass upstairs and get ready. For me. Please," Sarah said, knowing her pleading would motivate him.

Billy gave in to her begrudgingly and moved toward the stairs with body language matching a child put in a time-out. He did love her, even though he hardly showed it in his actions. The sound of heavy feet filled the room as he made his way up the stairs. He reached the bedroom and removed his oil-stained shirt. He sat down at the edge of the bed away from his wife and the sounds of the activity in the kitchen.

Billy did feel something. It was sadness and remorse. He had been failing so much for so long at so many parts of his life that he had forgotten what it was like to care. He did care, but it was so far down in his soul, layered under years of neglect for his own well-being and those around him. The depression crept in slowly at first, like a shadow on the ground. He briefly allowed himself to think back to when he was a better person.

He remembered his childhood before his father's death. He remembered those around him who held him in high regard. Some of them would be at the party. He lowered his shoulders as he thought of what his mother might say to him that night.

His mother had experienced the worst of his reactions to his father's death. She had witnessed his depression and his descent from a happy child to the wrinkled young man he had become. Billy knew his mother's love. It would have been enough for most kids, even after the death of a father, but Billy had shared a special relationship with his dad, and there was nothing his mother could have done to stop his attitude and demeanor from unraveling.

"I don't hear the shower," Sarah shouted from the bottom of the stairs.

Billy did not want to continue his thought pattern. It was very simple to feel sorry for himself—to return to happier days, when his father was there at arm's length. So, like always, he blocked out his feelings and thoughts of a different past. It was easier for him to have no feelings than to dwell on what might have been. When

Sarah called to shake him into getting ready, he was brought back to reality and effortlessly went back to his normal performance: a man with no heavy attachments to this world, even though he had a loving wife and three children who needed him as much as he needed his own father.

As he tossed the oil-stained shirt into the hamper, he briefly looked up, almost unto the heavens, and wished for things to be different. It was a moment of weakness for Billy. He had not prayed to God since his father passed. He was not sure what his beliefs were anymore. He had felt anger toward God for taking his father. Rather than make it complicated or blame God, he simply dismissed the presence of God altogether.

But for a small moment as he looked up, he wished his father wouldn't have died or maybe even more so that he was able to have a better relationship with his own kids and could be to them what his father had been to him. *Silly*, he thought, and he headed into the bathroom.

All his life Billy had hated the beginning of a shower. The unknowing was agonizing. Was it going to be hot, cold, or just the right temperature? He didn't spend time thinking about why he hated it, but he knew it bothered him. He would turn the shower on, then he would reach in and check the temperature with his hand. He would wait a minute or so, wasting water, and check it again. Finally, he would step into the shower once he knew it would not be a shock to him—too hot or too cold.

This time he was about to check the shower with his hand. He pulled back the curtain a little and began to reach his hand into a position under the water. His hand would reveal if he could step in and shower or if he needed to wait for it to warm up further.

"Get moving, Billy," Sarah called to him again.

He pulled his hand back so he was not touching the water any longer. He grabbed his towel off the rack, put it on the floor next to the base of the shower, and turned on the shower's overhead light. He stepped into the shower at the end furthest from the showerhead, as he was unable to complete his test, and prepared to step under the cascade of water.

Billy thought of all the times he had taken a shower and been so cautious about the water temperature, yet here he was, scurrying to get ready. It was not like him to break his own monotonous patterns. It must have been the thoughts about wanting and wishing to be a better person. Where were these thoughts coming from? He did not normally think reflectively. His existence was as simple as possible.

He entertained the thought that maybe he could change and realized how strange the feeling of positive daydreaming was to his psyche. He fleetingly imagined the smile on his wife's face from seeing him rather than a look of pity or frustration. He paused a few extra moments, hoping the shower would be warm enough, and stepped under the water. It was sharp and cold. Instantly, sound and light and all other things picked up by senses went from large and discernible to small and imperceptible. A sharp, quick pain hit him like lightning in his head, and a moment later he felt nothing.

* * *

Billy awoke with a sensation of a gentle breeze and warmth rolling over him. He was standing, or at least he thought he was standing. There was wind hitting his face, and the sun was shining on him as he recognized its warmth on his shoulders and forehead. He could not see or hear anything. He could feel though. His feet were on something loose and rocky. He had shoes or sandals or something like that on his feet.

He put his hands to the ground, and he imagined he was on gravel or stones. As he made this discovery, a dull light came to his eyes and grew stronger with every second. His ears began to recover and back up what his feet and hands were telling him. He could hear the loose stones beneath his feet as he moved them and could hear the wind rolling over other objects around him that he could not yet see.

He struggled to understand at first. Where was he? He was just in the shower, trying to get ready for the party. Did he slip and hit his head? Was he dreaming or unconsciously imagining what was happening to him? Perhaps the house was struck by lightning, or aliens had abducted him. He laughed at the shows about aliens as he wasted so much time watching them on television.

Regardless, he had never appreciated his full senses before this moment. He needed to be able to fully see and hear his surroundings. Without his sight, he feared to move. He thought, *If I am on a cliff and take one step, I would fall to my death.* The presence of the stones frightened him and brought all kinds of perilous scenarios to his mind. He could be in a gravel parking lot and might walk into a moving car. He may be on a trail, and bikers might not see him, or an animal might attack. He questioned his sanity. He assured himself it was a dream and not reality. Clearly, he was not in the shower. This took him back and forth between the realms of where he was presently and where he came from. Was this real or not? Where in the hell was he standing?

As his frustration grew, and he became more and more impatient for answers, his eyes could now make out fuzzy, vague shapes. He saw a lot of large rocks at first, and his ability to see became more acute. He could make out the smaller rocks and gravel that lay beneath his feet. He was safe. He was not standing before a dangerous drop.

All his senses were now nearing normalcy, and he realized he was in a vast wilderness. It was a desert. Not a desert that one thinks of like the Sahara, where sand dunes roll like ocean waves. It was a rocky and desolate desert. Limited and sparse vegetation grew among the rocks. Thorny and worn bushes littered the landscape, and small patches of dead or dying grass sporadically emerged from the stone covered under foot.

He laughed as he thought back to not testing the water in the shower. He must have gone into shock from the water being too hot or too cold. Billy felt vindicated. All those years of testing the water in the shower were now justified.

He decided to sit down on one of the rocks and gather his thoughts. Fiercely trying to remember details about what happened, he remembered that sound and light were virtually sucked out of the bathroom in an instant. There was an instantaneous pain in his head he remembered as well.

It was almost like a scene from *Stars Wars*. He chuckled at his nerdy science-fiction reference, but he realized something like that may have happened to him. Somehow he traveled to where he now sat, faster than the speed of light, like Han Solo and Chewbacca. The difference was, he did not throw some levers or push any buttons. Something had brought him there to that desert. Reaching for answers, he remembered he did look to the heavens for a moment and wished for change.

No! he thought to himself.

That was a crazy thought. He hadn't prayed in a long time, but one glance to the heavens and a brief thought hurdled him to this place? But then again, he was sitting on a rock in the middle of the wilderness. What exactly was the definition of *crazy* to a man who had lost his senses in the shower, only to find himself where he sat?

Then there was another matter to contemplate: He was wearing clothes and the sandals he had suspected earlier when he could not see them. The clothes he had on were not his; he wasn't even wearing his potato chip oil–stained blue shirt. What he had on looked like the clothing of a shepherd or Jesus's father, Joseph, from a bad Nativity play.

He was faced with both quandaries: How did he get there, and where did these strange clothes come from?

Billy heard something moving in the large rock outcropping behind him. He saw a scaly black shape between two medium-size rocks. It was a black snake. The situation no longer called for contemplation. He jumped to his feet as fast as his eyes spied the slithering creature.

The snake was aggressive and struck out at him. Billy jumped away from the rock and back onto the loose stones. The snake seemed to retract into the rocks as Billy moved away, but then it launched out at him again when he leaned toward it to get another look. The snake made sounds like both a snake and a human as it lurched in his direction. Billy leaned against the rocks to test if the snake was really saying something, or to see if he was imagining the entire thing.

"Flee," it seemed to say, hissing as it struck. "Flee."

Billy found this very odd. Was the snake talking to him as it tried to bite him? He really questioned his sanity now. The sun was directly over his head when he looked up to acknowledge its warmth on his face and shoulders. Grateful he had full use of his senses, he thought he would at least have the sun to help him gain basic navigation and direction. He was thankful for his sight, which would allow him to find his way and avoid any other snakes or animals the wilderness might reveal. When the sun moved, it would gradually shift west, and he would at least have direction.

Now he knew why the snake was telling him to flee. As he looked around, he noticed something camouflaged prior to that moment. Clearly his eyes were not totally corrected just yet. A large cat lay perched, looking at him just thirty yards from the escarpment of rocks where he was attacked by the snake.

A cheetah or leopard lay on a tremendous boulder, resembling the sphinx. He knew it to be one of the two based on the spots, but his eyesight was still in question as he tried to discern which animal faced him. In his defense, it was hard to know which it was, as the spots and coloring of the beast blended in perfectly with the rocks and background.

He was in danger again from an animal. Minutes separated the two events. Billy went from taking a shower to being in the wilderness. He went from having all his senses to having none of them to having all of them back again. And now he went from being snapped at by a fierce snake to being stalked by what he now knew to be a leopard. He realized this as the leopard rose; its head and body were much larger than a cheetah. Although he was in danger, he admired the beauty of the animal and the way in which it moved.

As a young boy, he saw all nature in great admiration. His father had taught him to respect and love all living things. Looking up at the sun, which hadn't moved, he realized there was only one thing to do: He had to escape the two things in this landscape that threatened him. He started walking away from the snake among the rocks and more importantly the leopard that was moving toward him. Billy was in motion and began to flee as the snake directed.

CHAPTER 2

HUNTER

Careful to avoid drawing attention to himself, Billy took a light, quick pace away from the leopard. The cat appeared to be pacing him. The predator was not going faster or slower than his quarry, but was pushing him in a purposeful direction. Billy kept moving. After five minutes, over very similar terrain spotted with rock outcrops that made maneuvering difficult, Billy stopped, out of breath. He thought the cat may have given up on him, as it was no longer in sight.

Just then it emerged from behind a larger wilted bush, announcing its presence again. It kept the same pace and distance as before, guiding Billy in a certain direction. Billy wondered if the animal was stalking him to tire him out, or perhaps worse—pushing him to another cat that would assist with the kill.

Though he had a vague knowledge of big cats from nature shows, as he moved, he could not remember specific hunting tactics of big cats—more specifically, leopards. Either way, Billy was in exceptional peril and kept moving. As he scurried, he realized this was more exercise than he had done in the last five years. He was in terrible shape. He struggled amid the rocky terrain and stumbled trying to keep his footing. It was difficult to keep an eye on the cat and move forward at the same time. Luckily for him, the leopard was content with the simple pace and would only match Billy's speed. This allowed Billy to slow down occasionally if the activity was too taxing. Billy found the limited attack of the big cat to be forgiving, and he thought the leopard must pity him, thinking he was an easy mark. He thought his younger self would do a lot better in this situation. He was also struggling to maneuver in the sandals. He had never worn a pair of sandals in his life.

He was such a good athlete as a youth. He participated in every sport available to him. He played football, basketball, baseball, and occasionally ran track or wrestled when time would allow. Though he never played tennis in a league or tournament, he and his friends played it competitively at the park near his house. Now he was struggling to out speed walk a leopard in a desert wilderness. Billy was an out-of-shape, thirty-year-old man who was in the middle of a death struggle. He was physically unprepared for the challenge. After all these years of wasted time on the couch, his lack of passion and energy was potentially going to be the end for him.

Billy remembered being told by heart attack survivors and people who had diabetes that they wished they had been more active or done more to improve their diet. They said getting the diagnosis made things real. All they could do was get in better shape and eat healthier moving forward. Billy did not have that kind of time.

He was out of shape and had mere moments before the cat ended his life. A heart attack might happen as he tried to get away, and he may have diabetes, but that was irrelevant if the cat was going to eat him. The chase was killing him mentally and physically. He was planning a visit to the doctor in his mind if he were to return home from wherever he was. And then he was going to join a gym.

What a waste of talent from his younger days. He stopped playing sports when his father passed. His father was his biggest fan and supported everything he did, even outside of sports. His father threw balls for him at batting practice, passed him the football, and helped him with his jump shot. But presently, he was about to be eaten by a predator because he was an all-conference potato chip eater who trained on the couch daily. He would need to find a ray of light in this situation. He needed to find a positive thought that would allow him to deal with this untenable set of circumstances.

A fresh thought popped into Billy's head. It was a hope. There must be something in front of him that could save him. It was a possibility. A cat could climb a rock better than he could, so he was not looking for a place to get up onto for safety. Perhaps he could climb on a rock if he could find a branch or large stick and fight the cat off as he tried to leap, but there were very few trees, if any, close to him. He would look as he kept pace with the animal.

The one positive thought that kept coming to him was he imagined water, like a lake or river, ahead in the wilderness. He also imagined civilization in front of him. Either might work to deter the cat from continuing his attack. Though some cats, like leopards, panthers, and jaguars, did not mind water and could thrive in it, maybe this cat would think him not worth the trouble of going into a body of water and getting wet. Water might save him. What about other people? He was in the wilderness, but there had to be other people there. Those two thoughts gave him hope. He would keep his eye open for water. He would keep his eye open for people and civilization. In the meantime, as he moved, he began looking for something he could use to defend himself.

Billy did not want to die. He recognized the familiar competitive drive and spirit he thrived on as a youth. He almost tasted the thick competition between himself and the cat. The cat was not going to win. The leopard was not going to beat him. The original Billy was back and ready to contend. Like so many times when he was younger, and the game was on, there was no one better than Billy to be in the middle of this situation. Small thoughts about the "why" of his presence there popped in and out of his head, but he constantly refocused on his adversary, the search for water or civilization on the horizon, and for any kind of weapon. Energized with survival and adrenaline flowing through him, Billy would not surrender to his opponent.

Another unforgotten but equally unpracticed feeling emerged as well. He sensed faith. Billy was recently unaccustomed to its power and strength, but he felt it nonetheless. At first it was faith in himself and what he could do. He then sensed a stronger feeling.

It was kick-started by the brief moment he looked to the heavens before his shower. Was this the faith he knew as a boy coming back? The idea that God had not abandoned him and that an almighty deity cared for him emerged as a thought. He felt faith in what he could do and that a power stronger than himself was still active in his life.

Billy kept an eye on the beast as he moved, making sure he was not being tricked or out flanked. Constantly moving forward, he occasionally looked up to see if the sun was starting its descent in the west, but it seemed to stand still. Without a watch, he could not tell how long he had endured the encounter with the cat. His determination and ambition to live grew with every step. He was focused on his purpose to survive, but at times he would think about his life—his life back before he stepped into the shower. His life before he walked up the stairs. His life wasted on the couch. He had a wonderful and beautiful wife, whose life revolved around him. She would do anything for him and had stood by him through so much. She was with him through his melancholy and depression. She was with him even though he went from job to job and had been fired a couple of times. She was with him as promotions came and were never to reach fruition. Most of his employers stated he had no passion and lacked energy in his reviews.

She stood by him as friends would come in and out of his life. It was almost as if many of them wanted to be his friend and identified the potential of what may lay under the surface of his downhearted demeanor. He sincerely felt sadness for not treating her better and for the time he wasted not showing her his love. Billy thought about his children: Teddy, Alison, and Bryce. What did they do to deserve a distant and cold father? He thought about relationships and friendships that were thwarted by his own sabotage, like Steve, his childhood best friend.

He wished he was in front of all of them right now. He imagined the desert wilderness as a large arena—his family; his employers, both former and present; friends who were currently in his circle and those who were out; people from the community; and random other spectators. They were there in the crowd, watching the event. Billy versus the leopard. He would finally show them his true self.

No longer the man who lacked ambition, he was the man reborn, baptized in his own sweat, as it was getting increasingly warmer with the sun seemingly not moving and with the activity of the chase. Billy saw his father in the crowd with a smile across his face. His father was proud. For so many years, he was ashamed his father might be looking down on him with disapproval. His father certainly did not want him to be a man without drive or passion.

Billy's father was a model for all other fathers in the community. Al was a great father and husband. He thrived in the community as a businessman and philanthropist. Billy was going to survive this and beat the leopard for all of them, but especially for his dad.

Billy thought if he became half the man his father was he would repair and restore all the broken relationships in his life and contribute to the community he had neglected so thoroughly.

Billy's father was incredible. He put Billy in front of everything. He saw his friends' fathers unable to come to ball games or absent at family and school events because of work, laziness, or simple selfishness. Billy was extremely lucky.

As he struggled for survival, Billy wished he could have five minutes with his kids to touch their bright faces, hug them, and give them a taste of what his father had shared. He wanted to go into the backyard and play catch with each of them—to smile as they improved various skills and to help them make adjustments on what they did not do well. Billy wanted to be involved in their lives again. He wanted to be a part of their triumphs and failures.

These were not specific thoughts. They were vague and general, but they were happy and positive. He had not felt those feelings for a long time. It was funny he felt these feelings as he was being stalked by a killer. Then again, perhaps it was the perfect thing to think about, as the idea of being eaten in the wild was a dark possibility. He longed to ask them about their days and to know their friends and interests. He saw each of them in the stands of the arena, cheering for him and adding positivity to a bleak situation.

Those kids needed a father like he had, even though he may have only had his dad for a short time. A touch of graciousness came over Billy. How self-absorbed he was to pity himself over his father's passing when other kids may not even know their fathers. Or like his situation, know their fathers but have them be the opposite of what a good pop should be.

He experienced so much more than others with his father. It seemed sinful to have been so angry about losing him. In fact, he should have been grateful for the time awarded to him, as his father's love was rich and abundant. His father's love was thicker than some people have experienced in a lifetime, even though it was short lived.

Billy had been an inattentive father. He had been a careless husband. Billy did not know what had happened to him in the shower, but he knew if he was able to return to his former life and world he would no longer be the husband and father he was before this happened. Change was eminent. He would be a better man. He felt as though he was already a better man, and he would continue to improve.

He would get on his feet and engage with the world again—the small world that included his wife, children, and community. The larger world involved everything else and his faith. He resolved to be better. His renewal was dependent on his survival in the wild and presently, by not being eaten by a large spotted cat that matched his pace whether fast or slow and never seemed to try and overtake him, merely push him. What was he pushing him toward?

In the distance, on the ground ahead, there was something

noticeably strange—an anomaly or irregularity on the landscape's floor that shone in the sun. Billy hoped it was metal. Could it be a weapon or something he could shield the cat off with on top of a rock? A new hope filled his heart.

The shining object, or objects, in front of him became another possibility that would allow him to continue. Running low on energy, Billy recognized the feeling of dehydration. When younger, all athletes know to get water in their system before, during, and after a contest or workout. At some point, all athletes experience not having enough liquid in their system on an extremely hot day or during a very rigorous workout, game, or program.

Some athletes fall into this trap because of circumstance; others just don't drink enough water or other liquids. It starts with a headache and then leads to muscle cramps. Billy remembered an instance in which it happened to him during a cold football game in late October. He never thought he would get dehydrated in cold weather, so he did not think to replenish his fluids. He cramped up so badly at the end of the second quarter that he could barely play to start the second half.

His father, as always, was there with help and advice, giving him a banana, which aided in the recovery, as well as the water he drank to get back to normal. At present, though, he was thirty years old and sweating a lot. The sun added to the rigorous battle against the cat. He would need to find water to potentially thwart the cat but also to get fluids in his body.

Eventually, he would pass out from the lack of fluid in his body, and the leopard would win. Billy contemplated that the cat would be in a similar situation, but he also knew this was where the cat lived, and it knew where there was water and most likely was better suited and adapted for this type of cross-country challenge. He only had a soda and some potato chips in his stomach from hours earlier, and he was wearing unfamiliar sandals—not exactly the kind of sustenance one needs in this type of life-or-death struggle and hardly the footwear of an athlete.

If Billy was to change completely, he would not only need to fix the problems in his life that dealt with people but he would also need to fix the way he lived and took care of himself. Having low self-worth for so long and having thought so little of the effect his behavior had on his family and friends, he did not think he needed to eat well or exercise. His poor eating habits and lack of physical activity were an act of sabotage that would slowly lead him to the grave.

He decided he was going to be good to himself, if given a second chance. He would listen as his wife discussed superfoods, vegetable servings, and moderate consumption of sugar and fats. He was out of shape, and every step he took reminded him of this hard fact. He did very little to help his health and did a lot to hurt his well-being. Another resolution: he would not only do better to those around him but to himself and his body as well.

He was closer to the shining object in front of him. From this vantage point, he could see it was not metal. He could see it was very white. It was the sun-dried carcass of an animal, perhaps a deer or gazelle, exposed for much longer than he was, but it made him realize his own mortality. The scene was vicious and savage.

There was a good chance the animal was killed and eaten by the same leopard that was after him now. He did not want his bones scattered in this desolate place on the ground among the snakes and rocks. The constant bombardment of the sun and sandy winds made the ivory shiny and gave it a luster that mimicked metal from a distance. He was disappointed it was not a knife or a spear or anything that could pierce the hide of the leopard or something that could fend it off.

Billy realized some of the ribs had sharp ends. He stopped and bent over to pick up two of the ribs. Moving over to a large stone, he made sure there were no snakes, and he began to sharpen the ends. His goal was to fashion a knifelike weapon. If he could take one of the larger bones and use it like a club, he would be a double threat against the beast. He could stab at him with the sharp rib and fight off the cat with the larger bone.

The first rib he tried to sharpen cracked under the pressure of his efforts. The second rib did the same. He took care the third time to find a bony rib that was denser and thicker. The entire time the leopard was getting closer. The third attempt proved to be fruitful, and he now had his first weapon. He looked among the scattered bones for part of a hind leg that could be used as a club. It was larger and easy to find. He was now a real gladiator in the arena, with weapons and tools to fight and defend.

When he had stopped to make the weapon, the leopard did something Billy did not expect. The cat jumped onto a medium-size rock and lied down after coming dangerously close to him initially. It almost seemed that the cat was watching him like it was interested in the process of making the weapon and bored with the chase. It was possible the leopard needed a break and brief respite.

Maybe the cat thought Billy was not going anywhere, and no matter what weapon he created there would be meat in his belly. Billy appreciated the act of kindness, if that was the case. He was able to take a minute to sit down and make sure no snakes, scorpions, or any other wild animals were going to attack.

Since he was able to see and hear again, every experience he had with animals there involved danger. He was being extracautious. If the cat was going to allow him to take a break, he would, but he sat on the rock with his club and handmade blade ready to kill anything that was thinking about killing him. He did not know how long he had to rest but was going to take advantage of the cat's generosity.

The beautiful leopard raised up to stretch out, revealing that a male was tracking down Billy. Billy assumed it was a male, but the obvious physical appendage made things clear. The fact that the cat was a male did not change anything about the severity of the situation, but it allowed Billy some strange insight into what he was up against.

In the wild, female and male leopards are equally fierce, and the danger of being attacked and eaten really makes the classification irrelevant. If with cubs, a female would perhaps be more dangerous, as it would not allow any harm to come to its nursery. It would most likely respond by tearing a threat's head off to protect the cubs, which is what this leopard male was probably looking to do regardless. The large cat was up and moving toward him.

"Nap time is over," Billy said out loud to himself as he raised his new weapons to show the cat, who abruptly turned away and started moving again.

Billy was sore. After all that movement and exercise, he almost regretted stopping to rest. He was sluggish and lethargic from being out of shape, thirsty, and hungry. His feet hurt from the gravel and uneven terrain, and the sandals clearly did not help the matter. What he wouldn't give for a nice pair of sneakers.

The leopard was so smooth and sleek as it moved. Billy had begun to revere the animal. He had so much experience on the couch watching television. As a go-to, he would watch nature shows on Animal Planet and National Geographic when a good movie could not be found. He certainly watched a lot of programs about big cats, many of them being on late at night. He would stay up late watching the programs, unable to sleep.

He knew that leopards existed in various parts of the world and knew that some leopards, panthers, and jaguars lived in remote parts of the world, isolated and reclusive. Judging by the geology, geography, and terrain, he began to put together that he may be in North Africa or the Middle East, but he couldn't be sure. The landscape was rugged and unforgiving wherever he was, and as he continued to move he felt his muscles and joints start to loosen and become less constricted from his brief rest. His eyes scanned the horizon for water or civilization as he returned to developing ways to get out of this struggle.

Billy considered that the cat may have no interest in attacking just then. Maybe the cat was merely curious. There were no other humans for the miles. Maybe the animal had never seen a bipedal creature.

"Why are you doing this?" Billy exclaimed. "Do you really want to kill and eat me, or is this just a game?" he yelled out to the beast.

The cat stopped and sat both times when he cried out to him. The leopard initially sat down the first time he yelled, got up, and then moved toward Billy afterward and then sat down again when Billy spoke. It then moved toward Billy again when words stopped coming out of his mouth. Questioning why the cat would stop and listen, he continued to move because the cat was moving quickly toward him.

Billy thought about all the new revelations he came to regarding his family, friends, and health. Here it was in front of him. His life would end in that barren wilderness in the clutches of a leopard. He would never see his kids again. His wife would never know his true feelings and dear sentiments. He would never reconnect with friends or engage with the community from which he came. He would never get a chance to get into shape and work on his health.

The leopard quickened its pace and surged toward him. Billy raised his bony defenses and prepared to clash with the cat. The leopard did not attack, however. It moved off to the left behind Billy. Billy's senses again came into play. He heard and smelled water. As he swung around 180 degrees, he saw where the cat had gone. All four of his paws were submerged in a river. The long tongue of the cat lapped up the water into his mouth, flushing over its powerful jaws—the jaws that Billy thought would crush his skull.

Billy quickly moved down to the river. He needed a drink and momentarily set fear aside, as both he and the cat were preoccupied anyway. With the cat on his left, Billy used one eye to make sure the cat was not going to be deterred from getting a drink. With the other eye, he guided his cupped hands into the water to pool refreshment to his own mouth.

After getting his fill, the cat turned away from the water, ran across some loose gravel and sand by the river's edge, and started to return from where they came. Stopping between some large rocks, the cat looked back momentarily, licked his right paw, and raised it across his nose, where water from the river still dripped. It was almost as if the leopard was saying farewell.

Billy raised his hand, waving, and said, “Thank you for not killing me,” as the leopard skillfully leaped off toward the rocks.

Down the river in the distance, Billy saw people. There was a gathering of close to fifty or more a hundred yards away. Billy could not tell what they were doing, but it looked as if one man was in the river, and people were looking or listening to him. Perhaps this was his chance to get some answers as to where he was and what he was doing there.

He began walking down the bank of the river toward the crowd. He looked back one more time, and there was no sign of the leopard. Billy felt a sense of both relief and accomplishment. He had survived. The water left a funny aftertaste in his mouth. Billy had never had river water before. If it were good enough for the cat, it was good enough for him. Both gladiators went their separate ways—one back to the wilderness and the other toward some strange folks down by the riverside. He had survived.

CHAPTER 3

BAPTIZED

As he approached the group of people, Billy was confused by the sound of their voices. From what he heard and from what he could discern, there were two or three languages being spoken by those gathered. None of them were speaking English. He was right to believe he was not close to home. The value of senses was still on Billy's mind from before, but he was frustrated, thinking his senses meant nothing when the information being received by them was unintelligible. Briefly having his sight, hearing, and smell gone and then restored made him agitated. After his arduous journey in the wilderness and his escape from the snake and the leopard, he now found civilization, but he could not understand anyone, and they most likely could not understand him.

Listening to them speak was like walking around in the dark. He occasionally understood a few words, and by their actions he assumed the gathering must be a religious ceremony. Several of them, with both hands, reached to the heavens and spoke to the sky. Most of the crowd was on the other side of the river across from him, on their knees or sitting with their legs crossed, muttering something. Even if he could understand what they were saying, it would be difficult, as they were speaking quickly. With so many talking, it was hard to follow one of them at a time.

Billy sat down on the riverbank and watched the people intently, hoping to discover a clue or a piece of information that would further his understanding of where he was or what had happened to him. The leader of the group stood out to him. He was not wearing the same clothes as the rest of the people. He was wearing what looked like animal hides, light in color and rough to the touch. Billy was reminded of Grizzly Adams as he examined the man's face.

A full beard and long wavy hair shot out in several directions, giving him an unkempt look. He appeared to be a man of the wilderness and one who could catch a leopard chasing him and snap its neck. He stood waist deep in the river. Judging by the way those gathered treated him, he was their leader or a conveyor of information.

The grizzled man then took one of the reverent individuals with one hand to the back and the other near his belly and immersed him into the river while saying something adamantly. The man emerged gratefully and hugged the bearded man while tears flowed from his eyes. Billy had been to a baptism of an adult born-again Christian after he and his wife had just married.

They were looking for churches to join and were invited to a ceremony. The ceremony Billy witnessed prior to the one unfolding in front of him did not seem to have the same energy or spirituality that this one did. The man draped in animal skins was something different. His charisma and energy seemed to add to the sun's glow upon the river, and for a moment it radiated back upon him, giving him a heavenly and angelic gleam.

Until this time, Billy was a bystander. He sat quietly on the other side of the river while other members of the group were baptized with the river water or prayed zealously. He still continued to struggle with understanding what they were saying. Then, without warning and almost as if someone had whispered in the leader's ear, the man gave a strange look at the others and then directed his gaze on Billy.

His eyes were deep and piercing. The wild man's eyes stood out because his facial hair covered so much of his face from mustache to beard. It seemed like his eyes were two blue islands in a sea of facial hair. Billy felt almost as uncomfortable with him noticing him as he was when the leopard pursued him. Billy was just pledging to be a better husband, father, and member of his community, but this was not his community, and he did not know this man or understand his words. Billy became the unsure and passive man from before the encounter with the leopard. He did not want to be noticed.

The man extended his arm toward Billy and smiled. He then moved his fingers in unison toward Billy in what assumedly was a gesture to arise and come to him. Reluctant to get up after his ordeal with the leopard, Billy got to his feet and came to the edge of the water. Billy looked at the rugged man in front of him and for unknown reasons waded into the water. He did not want to be noticed, but the man had an unusual charisma about him. His demeanor and especially his passionate eyes eliminated fear and concern.

The river was gently moving past him and became knee deep, then waist deep, then almost as high as the bottom of his chest. Billy struggled, made it through the deeper middle, and regained his footing. The water level went down as he drew closer to the wild man. First to his stomach, then his waist, and then to his knees. He was now standing right in front of the bearded stranger.

The stranger reached out with both hands toward Billy. Billy withdrew at first. The man gave him a look of assurance. Billy did not think the man wanted to do him harm, just as he learned that the leopard did not have ill intentions in the end. He allowed the man to take him into his arms. The man lowered him into the river.

Billy was completely immersed in the water. Under the gentle moving river, he thought he heard something. He thought he heard beautiful voices singing. It sounded angelic. He could only liken it to the sound made on Christmas Eve by a choir. He could not understand the words and could not place the melody or song that was being sung, but he heard the beauty, and he was thankful for hearing it. Billy opened his eyes and saw rays of bright yellow-and-white light shooting in from above into the water. It looked like a thousand powerful flashlights were shining into the river.

Combined with the heavenly music, Billy thought that all of what he was experiencing was a dream. He had never heard or seen such beauty. Billy was brought from the water and made upright again. As he emerged from the river, he understood all the words said by the group of people around him. It no longer sounded like they were speaking in foreign languages. They also understood him because he was able to respond immediately.

"I baptize you for love and repentance, my son," said the wild man as he grasped Billy by the shoulders. "Did you hear the call to come to me—a voice in the wilderness?"

"I must tell you, I heard nothing calling me to you. A leopard attacked me miles away and drove me to the river," said Billy, out of breath. "I am not from here, and I have so many questions. I hope you can help me," Billy continued.

"I know you, and you know me. You have never been here before, but you know of it well. Earlier in your life, you heard my name, and you know of my story. Can you not think of who I am?" said the wild man.

Billy tilted his head to the side. Overwhelmed with emotion, fatigue, and frustration, tears fell from his eyes. He knew he was in the presence of John the Baptist from the Bible's New Testament. Afraid to speak in his presence and a reverence falling over him, Billy wept and put his hands to his face, ashamed. Billy knew of John the Baptist. He remembered that John was a servant to Jesus's coming in the Bible and ultimately was murdered on account of his loyalty, work, and affiliation. Reality was driven from Billy's current consciousness like the leopard drove him from the desert wilderness. What was this experience?

"Weep not, Billy. A wonderful blessing has been granted to you. First, you have experienced baptism in the Jordan River at a holy place. God has shown you favor. Second, Jesus Christ has also been here and knows you. He knows you are among us here currently. Jesus has been expecting you and wants to speak with you. He was right here where you stand many days ago," John said.

"Me?" Billy asked in awe.

"Yes, he blessed me by allowing me to baptize him as well. Jesus is truly humble for being of God. I asked that he baptize me, but he insisted I baptize him instead," said John as he moved out of the river and suggested Billy do the same with a wave of his hand.

"The Lord has blessed us with a beautiful day, and to conclude it he has given us the gift of a new friend," John said as he motioned to Billy. He continued to speak to those present. "Blessed be all who have come here to this holy place in search of God and his son. I have said to all who will listen that his coming was near, and now that Jesus Christ has been baptized he goes to finish his work. May we rejoice in his coming and the arrival of Billy. Their paths will cross again. Go with God, and may God bless you and grant you safe travels as you leave the wilderness and return to your homes."

Billy went to John and said, "John, may I call you John? I am not from here. I have come from another time and place. I am so confused by what has happened to me and why."

"As I said, I know you. The Lord has brought you here for a reason. You will have a difficult time here. You have already had a difficult time here. The Lord has not brought you here to die, so do not be afraid. The Lord has brought you here that you may benefit from new wisdom and change. Your will and patience will be tested as you proceed. But know this: you have been chosen for this unique experience because the Lord knows your true heart and can see into your mind. God knows your pain and wants to help you. Go with God through this journey, and trust in God's plan for you."

"I must be asleep, and this must be a dream," said Billy.

"Why do you doubt what your senses are telling you?" asked John. "You have been asleep and have had dreams before. Does this feel like a dream?"

"Not at all," said Billy with a look of confusion on his face. "Nothing I have experienced here has been like a dream, minus the fact that I am here!"

Billy watched as the people who had been there to see John left in different directions. He noticed none of them went the direction he had come from originally. Maybe some of them knew that way to be treacherous. Maybe they knew of the snakes and the leopards and the danger. Maybe the terrain itself was so dangerous, with the lack of water and absence of readily available food, that the idea of traveling through it was simply suicide. Clearly no one was from the barren place he had covered with the leopard. The people were headed toward civilization. He found the river before he found civilization, but both were strongly on his mind as he tried to out outmaneuver the leopard.

"John, you called this a holy place. What river is this?" Billy asked.

"You are on the banks of the Jordan River," said John.

"What is that called?" Billy asked as he pointed in the direction from where he came.

"That is the wilderness—the Judean Desert. I have wandered in the wilderness to get closer to God. It tested me and changed me for the better. You have survived that trial already. You will need the resolve and passion that allowed you to survive the wilderness in the days and months to come. Before your journey will be complete, you will be challenged mentally, emotionally, and physically. Seek Jesus Christ in this new journey. Don't give up on finding him, as your true future life will be revealed by your encounter with him and the journey that will lead you to him," John said with sincerity.

Billy looked at John sternly and said, "I am a stranger here. I can't explain what has happened, and I am afraid of what will happen next. I am alone here. Will you come with me? I could use your help in case I am unable to understand what people are saying again or if my senses fail me as before. You want me to find Jesus? He wants me to find him? I don't see how that will be possible! Where would I be headed? Forgive me if I doubt this plan and my ability to navigate!" Billy said angrily.

"When the black adder spoke to you saying flee, you doubted reality. When the leopard chased you to the Jordan River, you did not see the divinity of God's brushstroke. When you met John the Baptist and were baptized in the same waters as Jesus Christ, you still didn't feel the pull Jesus has on you like a magnet to metal.

"You doubt all these paranormal things because you have been living below normal, allowing nothing extraordinary to enter your life. Why should anything you have experienced here be unreal? I was chosen by God to prepare the way for Christ. I was told my coming was destined. God brought me here just as you were brought here. I have done what was prophesied. At first I questioned my purpose. I, too, did not believe I was in this reality, and soon this reality will come to an end for me. Perhaps if God sees me fit to return to my former life I will be grateful having been changed by the hand of God. No, I am not from your time or another time, but I was called to do this, as you are called to follow," John said.

When John revealed he was on his own journey and had learned from the experience, Billy was humbled. Billy was in the middle of a challenging day. John was putting his sandals on, and Billy realized he should have removed his when he went in the river. John had set them on the bank of the river while he was baptizing souls. As he put them on, Billy had a moment to reflect.

John was right. He had been living an extraordinary life. Billy thought, his town and the people in it were extraordinary. He thought, my wife and children are extraordinary. He failed to recognize that when he had all of it right in front of him. He had already changed in the brief time he was there. He wanted to be back home to make the most of what was extraordinary around him, but knew God had more plans for him and his metamorphosis was not complete.

John was right. He had been living an unexceptional life. Billy thought his town and the people in it were extraordinary. He thought his wife and children were extraordinary. He failed to recognize that when he had all of it right in front of him. He had already changed in the brief time he was there. He wanted to be back home to make the most of what was special around him, but he knew God had more plans for him, and his metamorphosis was not complete.

"John, I am ready to do as God wills," Billy said.

"You will be fulfilled when this journey ends," John said to him.

"Thank you for baptizing me. I was baptized as a baby, but it didn't have the effect of a baptism by John the Baptist. I believe in you. I believe in God and the plan that's in store for me. I believe in Jesus Christ and want to find him to complete my journey in this time and land. I have not believed for a long time, but I find myself in awe of you and the events of today," said Billy.

"Go with God, Billy," John said as he embraced Billy.

John asked Billy to walk with him back down the river. The river narrowed several yards ahead. At the narrowing, some large rocks protruded from the water. John leaped onto the closest rock on that side of the river. With two strides from one rock to another, he made it to the middle of the river.

John turned back to Billy and said, "Farewell."

A few more jumps and strides, and John was on the other side of the river.

"Will I see you again?" Billy asked.

"God will make that decision for us," said John as he headed up the riverbank.

Billy was shocked. At the top of the riverbank sat the leopard. John did not see the leopard. Billy yelled frantically for John to watch out. John paid him no attention and headed right toward the leopard. The leopard did not react. John reached the large cat and put his hand on its head, rubbing it as if the ferocious beast were a pet. John disappeared behind a tall rock. The leopard looked directly at Billy as if to say goodbye and then followed John into the wilderness.

Billy called out to John, "Which way did Jesus go? Where am I going?"

John responded from beyond the riverbank and shrubs. "Head north on the road west of the river. There will be several other pilgrims. Seek Bethsaida and Capernaum first. When you reach Capernaum, people will know where the Son of God is and what steps you are to take next."

Just then the cat reemerged and lurched on top of one of the rocks in the river as if to remind Billy this was serious, and he would push him again if necessary. Billy understood and headed up the riverbank in the opposite direction. The cat turned around and ran into the wilderness. Billy was putting faith in God after having been distant from God for all these years. Now his real journey was about to begin.

CHAPTER 4

FAITHFUL COMPASS

Billy was putting faith in God as John had suggested. He would let faith direct him. Faith had directed John in the wilderness, and now it would direct Billy. Billy did not need a leopard to push him now that he had faith. Having climbed up the riverbank, he emerged from some vegetation and saw a road that ran parallel with the Jordan River. There was not a lot of foot traffic on the road, but all the people on it were headed in the same direction.

Guided by instinct and a new faith, he got on the road and went with the flow. The sun finally showed movement. Billy questioned why the sun seemed to stay in the same place through the entire ordeal with the leopard, but he quickly squashed those negative thoughts, fighting to stay positive and have faith. God could obviously do amazing things, and he was experiencing one of them. He was in the middle of a paranormal miracle that had already challenged his senses, emotions, and physical condition.

He emerged victorious over those challenges in front of his family, community, and his father, as he used their imaginary presence as a tool to survive and compete. Now there was no leopard chasing him or a snake attacking him. Billy received advice from one of the greatest men in the Bible, John the Baptist, and was even baptized. He was ready for the next step in this unbelievable experience.

Billy could tell by the sun setting to his right that he was heading north on the road. After he was baptized in the Jordan River by John, and the voices and languages became clear, he was filled with new energy. Some of the energy came from the adrenaline and relief one might find after surviving a trek in the wilderness and being chased by a large carnivore, only to emerge unscathed. It takes a while for the body to readjust to simply walking for transportation as opposed to walking for survival. The adrenaline rush of all that had happened was beginning to wear off. His clothes were almost dry from the river, but his sandals were still soaked.

Billy realized he was starting to feel hungry. A new conundrum was before him: How would he find food to eat? As he walked down the road, he also realized he would need to sleep and perhaps find shelter. There was a lot on Billy's mind as he headed north.

The sun was beginning to set. It left a trail of stunning red, orange, and yellow dying embers as it transitioned to the edge of the horizon. Billy paused to compliment the moment. He could not remember the last time he took a minute to acknowledge something beautiful in nature or in his life. He remembered his daughter mentioning last week that there was a red fox on the side of the road as he took her to school. To her, it was a wonder. To Billy, it was another small, unimportant distraction.

Billy pretended he saw the fox and unemotionally said, "Oh yeah."

All his children were very good at spotting things in nature. Billy remembered when he went on a trip to a cabin on the lake with this father as a boy. They went fishing, kayaking, canoeing, and hiking. His father spent a lot of time showing Billy special little things. He would point out a blue jay or a weasel.

Right now he wished he was back in the car with his daughter. If only he could take a moment to let her know he had interest in what moved her. He would stop and look with his daughter, not only because the animal should be respected and is a part of the beauty of the world but that small moment would mean a lot to both of them.

It was a line that separated a parent and child. On one side of the line was trust, love, and consideration. On the other side of the line was disappointment and a lack of appreciation. Children sense the line even if they don't consciously acknowledge it. For that reason, he wanted to be back in his own time and place. He was putting faith in the direction of this quest, as he hoped it would lead him back to his real home. Home—where he could show his children that he would never be on the side of the line that caused a child to not be noticed or loved.

Billy was starting to get cold, and the feeling of hunger was becoming a lot more poignant. He saw that many travelers had set up camps on the side of the road for the night. Some of the camps were elaborate and had large tents and fires in front of them. Billy assumed those camps to be wealthy travelers, leaders, or officials. Other camps were very simple. He could see bodies and faces by the smaller fires. He wondered if one camp would take him in if he asked politely.

The cold was beginning to get to him after a long day in the heat and all the events that had led to this moment. His feet were still wet from the sandals, and they were cold too. He needed to rest, warm up, and eat. One of the camps, which was smaller and off to the left of the road, seemed to have less people. Billy walked closer to that side of the road in order to get a better look.

The fire and camp had one man sitting at it, facing the road as if he was expecting someone. Billy decided to approach the lone man. Billy hoped he would be a kind person willing to help him. He was a stranger in this land and had no idea if he would know this man's language. He knew he was able to talk with John, and he understood what was being said at the river, but would this man understand him? Would he understand this man? Billy was putting himself at some risk.

As he approached the fire, Billy saw the man quickly rise and reach for a sheathed sword. The man stood in an offensive stance, ready to remove the sword if needed.

"Announce yourself," the man said to Billy. "Who approaches, and what is your purpose?"

"My name is Billy. I mean no harm," Billy said, with his hands up to show he was not a threat. He was relieved the man could understand him.

"Come closer to the fire slowly," the man said.

"I saw your fire from the road and that you were alone. Are you taking company? I've had a challenging day. The warmth of your fire is my main interest. I have seen some of the animals in this strange land, and I am hoping your fire will not only keep me warm but protect us from their aggressive nature," Billy said, using the word *us* to help his plea for warmth.

The man motioned for Billy to come to the fire. He put his sword, still in its sheath, back where he had picked it up from on the ground next to the bags and other things he was traveling with. The firelight did not allow Billy to truly get a good look at the man's face.

"My name is Balthazar," the man said as he sat back down on what looked to be a blanket.

"I am Billy," he said, still being cautious as he approached the fire.

"Have you nothing with you as you travel? No food or something to sleep upon?" Balthazar asked.

"I am a stranger here in this land, brought here by a power much greater than I," said Billy. "I am not sure if I can explain what happened. You will think I am crazy."

"Please do not be hasty in judging me, and I will attempt to do the same for you as well. You will find I am not a judgmental person, Billy. My grandfather once traveled miles to see a baby born in a manger in Bethlehem not far from here, based on a prophecy and what he and his fellow magi saw in the stars," said Balthazar as he offered Billy some bread from one of his travel bags.

Balthazar came from a family of learned nobles who sought

wisdom among the stars and the world. His grandfather was also named Balthazar. His grandfather visited Jesus and his parents, Mary and Joseph, almost thirty years ago. Now too old to make the journey back to see the child grown into a man, his grandfather sent the Balthazar in front of the fire to seek Jesus and to gain his wisdom. Balthazar's grandfather described Jesus as one who would be wise and pious.

"My grandfather said that Jesus's coming was a prophecy and that all kings would bow before him. There are those who can foresee the future. They have been blessed with the power of prognostication," said Balthazar.

"Balthazar, I feel compelled to tell you what has happened to me based on what you have revealed," Billy said, looking apprehensive.

Billy was worried Balthazar would think he was strange and touched with craziness and run him out of his small camp. Billy took solace in the fact Balthazar was willing to share his food and fire, and that the revelation that he was related to one of the three wise men showed he understood that sometimes a star shining bright could be more than just a star. Billy was suddenly grateful for his Sunday school Bible studies as a child and countless Christmas pageants. The song "We Three Kings of Orient Are" would play in his head several times as he shared the fire with his new friend.

Billy decided to take a chance and tell Balthazar about his experience from the shower to the wilderness. He told him about the snake and the leopard. He described John the Baptist and his ministry of preparing the way for Jesus and how John had baptized him and Jesus shortly before him.

He described the sensations he felt under the water while being baptized and how when he came from the water he could speak and understand all the languages the people surrounding John were speaking. Billy then explained how John had given him a quest and a purpose. He told Balthazar that he was directed to find Jesus, as he had something important to tell him.

Balthazar sat quietly the entire time Billy described all of this and simply said, "Most likely, the snake was a black adder. Very common to these parts, and it has a nasty disposition."

Billy laughed and said, "I did not know how you would take my story. I expected you to drive me out of your camp. It is an unbelievable story, but it is all true."

"You have a device that brings water to you and washes you in your place and time," Balthazar said, always seeking wisdom. "The idea is ingenious."

"Yes, and until just recently it was one of my favorite things to do. Taking a shower is both relaxing and calming but it is also simple and efficient," replied Billy.

Billy thought Balthazar was not very interested in the unusual day and strange events that were described to him. How strange was Billy's story, and he only commented on the snake and the shower? He had clearly found a friend in Balthazar, and he was truthful in saying he was not one to judge. He was very fortuitous to stumble upon his new friend. Just as these thoughts passed, Balthazar offered him some dates and some salted meat. Everything tasted delicious to Billy. He was so hungry. He did not know how long he had been there or how long he was unconscious before he came to in the wilderness, so he tried to be polite. Yet he ate ferociously as his new friend offered him more food.

"I am truly grateful, Balthazar. You have been gracious and open-minded regarding my story. Thank you," Billy said with sincerity.

"As I told you, I am accustomed to peculiar events and happenings. My father spoke of my grandfather's trip and its significance to my family and the world. The man we are looking for is more than a man, but still a man. He is both the beginning and the end, as some have called him. Jesus is the Son of God, sent to earth," Balthazar said emphatically as he took a bite of bread.

"Did you say, your father spoke of your grandfather's trip? Does he no longer speak of it?" said Billy.

"My father does not speak at all. He is no longer with us, Billy," said Balthazar.

"I am terribly sorry, Balthazar. Did he pass recently?" Billy said cautiously.

"He died when I was twelve years old. I am now thirty, so eighteen years ago he left us," Balthazar said sadly.

"You and I have a lot in common, Balthazar. My father passed away when I was twelve as well. Do you mind me asking when you were born? Because it is my birthday today," said Billy, finding coincidence in all of this.

Balthazar paused without speaking. His mouth that still had bread in it was open. He finished chewing, swallowed, and said, "I was born today as well, my friend."

Both men sat quietly at the fire. One man was sent by his elderly grandfather to follow up on a story that began many years ago in a manger in Bethlehem. Billy understood the significance of Balthazar's quest and the weight of his grandfather's legacy. If only Balthazar could see the millions of Nativity plays performed at Christmastime each year and realize the true significance of his grandfather as the three wise men entered the stage.

The other man was in a queer place and outside of his realm of time, facing a task from John the Baptist to find Christ. Together they would have the same quest, essentially, and both reflected on the happenings in front of them. Each of them contemplated scenarios and occasionally shared their thoughts.

Either there were many events set in motion by a higher power in the world through time and space, or humankind simply fell into situations where there was no explanation. It was hard for Billy and Balthazar to imagine that God's divine influence and blueprint were not the creators of their situation.

"I would like it if we traveled together, Billy. It seems God has brought us together for a special purpose. Please be my guest tonight at my fire, as it is good and right for me to offer this to you. Eat as much as you want. But tomorrow we leave this camp not as host and guest but as partners," said Balthazar.

"I am thankful for your hospitality and grateful you have accepted me and my story," said Billy.

The two men with so much in common spent the next hour talking about the next day's travel and the amazing coincidences they shared. More than once they both shook their heads at the unique circumstances before them. They could have spent the entire night talking about things, but both were extremely tired. Balthazar reached into one of his travel bags and produced some more blankets for Billy to use. He truly was a gracious host. The men wished each other good night, Balthazar added a few pieces of wood to the fire, and they both laid down to sleep.

Billy turned away from the fire, facing the road and the river. He was tired but felt compelled to speak to God. It had been years since he had been in the practice of praying, but after the day's events and the strange chance coincidences between him and Balthazar, Billy felt the desire to try.

"Lord God, please hear my prayer," Billy whispered.

As a boy, Billy went to Saint Paul Church downtown. He had heard the pastor begin all his prayers with "Lord God, please hear our prayer." It seemed like a solid beginning, in case God wasn't listening. Judging by Billy's lack of prayer the last couple of decades, God was giving time to others who prayed more frequently and adamantly.

"I know we have not spoken much. I prayed for my father to survive his heart attack when they brought him to the hospital. I assumed you didn't hear me when he passed; otherwise you would have saved him. I was a foolish boy then. I am not sure I am done growing up yet, but I wanted to thank you for the time I had with my father. I want to thank you for my wife and my children. I want to thank you for the friends you have blessed me with. And finally, I want to thank you for my community and all the people who collectively have been a part of my life.

"I am praying now that you allow me to do right by them. If I am given the chance to go back to them, I want you to know things will be different. I will not waste my time and opportunities with each of them. I will make the most of those moments. And if I do not return, thank you for the opportunity to be a better person. I have been lost for so long. I am unaccustomed to these feelings of passion to chase after something. I hope you can hear me. Watch over us as we continue our journey. Thank you for Balthazar and his kindness," said Billy quietly as not to wake Balthazar.

"God hears you, my friend," said Balthazar, who was listening. "He hears you, and so do I. I could not have said a more committed prayer. God will certainly bless our travels. Good night."

"Good night, Balthazar, and thank you again for your hospitality," said Billy.

"As I said before, no longer mention it. Tomorrow we leave this camp as partners," said Balthazar.

The fire was warm against Billy's back. Billy combed over the day's events, trying to remember each thing in detail. He was excited for the adventure that lay before him, but he was still cautious after being attacked and chased. Billy was unsure of what had happened at the river with John the Baptist, but he knew he was blessed with being able to communicate with the people of the time and place. This fact would be paramount.

Billy had many random thoughts before he drifted off into a deep sleep. First, he thought about meeting John the Baptist and the potential of meeting Jesus Christ soon. Billy smiled and pulled the blanket over his shoulder. It was like meeting Mickey Mantle and Michael Jordan, Derek Jeter and Walter Payton. He hoped God was not listening to his thoughts, as he just compared Jesus to a Yankees shortstop.

Billy knew this was bigger than any baseball, basketball, or football player. Whatever was happening to him, he welcomed the gift and possibilities in front of him and was thankful to have a new friend to share this experience. Billy realized he had exercised and prayed in the same day. There was no way Sarah would believe it. He smiled as he thought of his wife and his children. As he fell asleep, their faces were his last thought.

CHAPTER 5

CAPERNAUM

The next morning both men rose rested and refreshed. Beside them the fire had burned its way to soot and lifeless ashes. Unfamiliar with Balthazar's habits, Billy wondered if they would be eating breakfast. Billy remembered that Balthazar said that when they left camp they would no longer be host and guest, but partners. They had not left camp yet, though, and Billy was unsure of where the new relationship began—on the road or right now. Before he could have that question answered, Balthazar handed him more bread and a small leather pouch.

In the pouch were grapes and dates. Balthazar explained that along the way south were numerous places where they could find grapes, dates, figs, olives, and more. Finding meat to hunt would be more difficult, but Balthazar told Billy that he had some money for provisions given from his grandfather's estate. His family has a worthy lineage of wealth and land. Balthazar told Billy that he would be welcome to live with him after their travels if God did not send him back to his own time. There were many jobs available for a man willing to work hard. Billy realized there was a possibility he might never go back. He tried not to think about that as he headed down the road with Balthazar.

"Why would God bring me here if not to better myself and return to my time?" Billy asked Balthazar. "My relationship with God is not as strong as it once was. But from what I know, punishment or reward for a life lived poorly or well comes in the afterlife of hell or heaven, not while we are here on earth. Am I being punished for not being a good father and husband?"

"I believe we must let our destiny reveal itself, the whole time trying to find that same destiny rather than manipulate or will it into happening. God has a plan for you. John the Baptist told you this was so. I believe John is connected to God and would not tell you something that was incorrect," Balthazar said. "We are just beginning our journey together. I have enjoyed your company thus far, but if you are going to whine and complain all the way to Jesus, I want to go back to last night and kick you out of the camp before you reached the firelight," Balthazar said and finished by laughing with boisterous enthusiasm for his own comedic effort.

Billy was happy to see Balthazar joking and laughing about what he said. Billy's life had been devoid of camaraderie and missing the simple joys of friendship since his father passed. If they were going to make it through this trip, they would need to keep positive and feed off each other's constructive emotions.

Billy was afraid he had been so upset and negative for so long his depressed side would come out more than he wished. He was determined to not allow those thoughts to enter his mind. He was grateful to have a new friend and was not going to push this one away as he had so many times before with melancholy and no reciprocation of friendship.

"As we begin our travels, I will give you bearings regarding our current position and direction. We are east of Judea and on the west bank of the Jordan River. We will be traveling north toward the Sea of Galilee. Our destination is Capernaum. It has been said that Jesus is in the Galilean region," said Balthazar.

"I know you are not from here, but I am assuming you have knowledge of this area from your grandfather's travels. I believe John the Baptist mentioned this is the direction Jesus would be traveling, but I am so grateful to have you with me. He did not say much more on the matter, and I am afraid I won't be much help."

"My grandfather had me study maps and routes growing up. This land is not where I am from, but I know it well. I know where to find water and where to find food and more. We have a good plan. When we get to Capernaum, we will find out if Jesus went through that town or if he is still there," said Balthazar.

The road to Capernaum was like an illustration from Billy's childhood Bible storybook. He remembered the pictures of Jesus on a donkey coming into Jerusalem, the tongues of fire on top of the disciple's heads at Pentecost, and a drawing of the Good Samaritan. All these memories were flooding his mind as they walked.

Balthazar was a solid companion, making sure to tell Billy about points of interest and fascinating things that were coming up ahead as they traveled. Billy was truly grateful for his friendship and company. Billy's father used to act similarly when they traveled. His own children would appreciate that kind of attention, and he was going to give it to them when he returned.

Billy had a friend named Steven when he was a boy who reminded him a lot of Balthazar. He had not thought of Steven in years. As a matter of fact, he had almost forgotten him. He wished Steven was there at that moment, or he was back in his own time so that he could seek out Steven. He wanted to know what he had been doing the last eighteen to twenty years. Billy wanted to know him again and share stories with him.

To have such a good friendship and lose it was a sin. A sadness overtook Billy momentarily as he thought about his inability to change anything back in his time, especially with his former friend Steven and his kids. He became immediately cheered up by a story that Balthazar was telling about a boy in his land who fell asleep on a camel as his family was traveling and had wandered two miles off course before they found him fast asleep while still on the camel plodding through the sand of the Arabian Desert. The boy was sternly punished for falling asleep and breaking off from the group. Balthazar thought it funny that the boy kept blaming the camel.

Billy smiled and recognized how similar in personality and demeanor Steven and Balthazar were. From what he remembered about Steven, if he couldn't see and only heard him tell that story he would have thought it was Steven grown up. Billy could not believe the similarities.

Physically they were very different, however. Steven was small for his age back when they were friends. Steven would always get banged up when they played football. Steven was tough, however, which made him twice his size in anything that was competitive. He could sense a similar toughness about Balthazar, like he showed the night before as Billy entered the camp.

Though Steven and Balthazar had very similar personalities and attitudes, physically they would not be comparable side by side. Balthazar was a taller man with a dark complexion. Billy thought it was strange to be removed from his time and space only to be here now with a man who reminded him so much of a childhood friend he now missed terribly after being reminded of him by Balthazar.

They had left early in the morning and were moving at a good pace. Billy looked above him several times and was relieved to see that the sun was moving normally and not sitting on top of him like it did when he was with the leopard. Billy was reluctant to ask Balthazar questions about the distance to Capernaum. He did not want to sound like his kids on a long trip, asking if they were there yet.

The sun was directly above them, and the temperature was warm. It was much warmer than it was that morning. Billy was starting to understand the current climate of the area—hot during the day and cool at night when the sun was gone. A desert climate. Deserts surrounded the river and the Sea of Galilee—the Sinai Peninsula, the Sahara Desert, the Arabian Desert, and the Judean Desert.

Billy realized his encounter with the leopard may have happened in the northern part of the Judean Desert. He started somewhere west of where they currently were and traveled northwest to John the Baptist. Now they were traveling north on the road parallel to the Jordan River on the way to Capernaum, which was on the northern tip of the Sea of Galilee, according to Balthazar.

Billy was not a good navigator. He never took enough time or care to be a good navigator. When his father was alive, Billy spent so much time listening and learning from his father. Navigation was not an inherited trait from his dad, however, though his father always knew where he was and where he was going. It was almost an extrasensory gift possessed by his father. But it did not transfer to Billy. And as Billy thought about the situation, it was a miracle he knew where they were and where they were going.

Balthazar pointed out that just in front of them was an area with a renowned natural spring, where the water was always cold, and there was a place just west of it that had wild grapes. Very few people knew of the secret vineyard. Everyone knew of the natural spring. Hundreds of people would travel to the spring every day. The water from the spring was fresh and cold and stayed cold long after the water had been taken from the spring. It was a blessing for weary travelers and for the herdsmen and people who were able to go there daily.

"This will be a good place to stop and rest. We can refill our water and then see if the grapes are undisturbed and ready to be eaten," Balthazar said as he lowered his water rations from his shoulders.

"Please let me carry some of that. Partners, remember?" said Billy as they made their way to the natural spring.

"I would have already given you a ration bag to carry, but they were running low, and it's no trouble. When we fill them up, and they are heavy, you can share the burden," Balthazar said, laughing. "You will appreciate the cool water on your shoulder as we travel in the sun."

"I am assuming it is about noon, Balthazar, based on the sun's position?" Billy asked.

"Noon? It is nearly midday, but I gauged the time of day based on my stomach's call to eat and no particular use of the sun!"

Balthazar was to be commended for his choice of stopping point. The water was cool on the tongue and extremely refreshing. Billy could have spent the whole day there relaxing in the shade of the palms and occasionally indulging in the splendid water. The two men had business to attend to, however, so it was off to the wild grape vineyard next.

Billy thought to himself that others would have picked the grapes clean by now if they were ready to be eaten. The distance from the spring to the grapes was a few miles to the northwest. Yes, it took them away from their goal of Capernaum, but Billy trusted that Balthazar had good motives, knowledge, and intentions.

The natural spring was well worth it. They were now refreshed and had replenished their water stored in the ration bags made of animal hides. The weight of the water was not cumbersome because the way the ration bags were balanced made the weight the smallest inconvenience. The grapes were just ahead of them.

"Billy, I must warn you, these grapes are delicious, but we must only take what we need. The reason there are always grapes available, is that those who live here and those who know of this secret place are not gluttonous. My grandfather was very clear in describing this blessing and how one is to appreciate it. Just as one might embrace forgiveness or graciousness. All are given by God and to be appreciated," said Balthazar.

"I understand."

Between two large rocks was a hidden opening to the place where the grapes were. There was an opening to the area that could only be described as an intricate collection of rocks, like the beginning of a maze. One rock went from south to north and jutted out like a cupped hand. The second rock went out from north to south one yard further. The rock arrangement made the entrance invisible to the naked eye.

Wanting to keep the entrance and location a secret, Balthazar looked all around to make sure no one was watching. The two men entered the opening in the rocks and followed the narrow path, which eventually opened into a grove. Billy watched Balthazar acknowledge the few other people there with respect. The honor they showed each other was noteworthy.

Billy then followed by acknowledging the few people there. The people they saw were gone as fast as they had been seen and Balthazar said a short prayer, took a bunch of grapes, and stepped back waiting for Billy. Billy did as his friend had done. He gave thanks for the grapes, borrowed Balthazar's short knife, and removed a bunch. Quickly they left back through the narrow passage and the strange entrance, making sure no one else saw.

Heading northeast, they took a shortcut back toward the road to Capernaum. They encountered some difficult terrain, and the sun was challenging. They were both lucky to be carrying the cool water, which never changed temperature. Billy thought the water may even be cold enough to use on his arm after he pitched in a baseball game.

Something about the water and the grapes revealed they were a blessing and very special. Billy found it strange that everyone shared in the little miracle of the natural spring. There was no fighting or greed. He found it equally strange that the people who knew of the secret grapes were able to keep it from the world, and he was impressed by the zealous nature in which they greeted one another. Also, they only took enough and did not take more.

Just then Billy took a grape from his pouch. He looked at Balthazar for approval. With a consenting nod, Balthazar blessed Billy's intentions. The grape was better than any grape he had eaten before. Balthazar smiled as Billy wiped his lips, enjoying the juice from the grape. Billy had full trust in his friend. Balthazar was a man who looked out for Billy as much or more so than he did for himself. Billy welcomed the friendship offered and would try to return the kindness at every opportunity. The men traveled until dusk and then camped. If they rose early and kept a similar pace the next day, it would take them to their destination in no time.

The two men had reached Capernaum. The size of the city was hard to gauge as it was spread out, but there were a good number of people there, as they were busy moving about. It was clear that fishing was a major part of the town's commerce as fishing nets were abundant near houses and the markets smelled of fish and the sea.

The Sea of Galilee lay just south of the city. Billy tried desperately to remember some of the Bible stories about the city or the body of water next to it. He remembered that Jesus had walked on water at the Sea of Galilee, but he struggled to recapture anything else that would be relevant. In a sense, if he had been a better Bible student when he was in Sunday school, he would have been a tremendous help to their search. He was a good student when he was young, but it really didn't help him now, as he had not picked up a Bible in the last eighteen years.

Balthazar said, "We will work faster if we split up. Let me go to the Sea of Galilee and you to the synagogue. Ask common people if they have seen Jesus. Be careful not to talk to anyone who seems to be wearing fine clothes or looks to be important. I am not sure what they think of Jesus. Some may not have the same feelings we have and will have negative motives. I will walk you to the synagogue, and then I will continue to the Sea of Galilee. I will meet you by the well just south of the city between the synagogue and the sea. If you find that Jesus is not here, come to the well immediately."

Billy nodded, acknowledging everything Balthazar had said. He had not thought of the perilous nature of their plan to look for Jesus, remembering that Jesus was eventually to be crucified by the people of this same land and the Romans who occupied it. Balthazar was wise to offer his warning.

Balthazar was able to find the synagogue easily and left Billy there to investigate. Certainly Jesus would have stopped at the synagogue on the way through the city if he stopped here, unless he and his people chose to bypass the city altogether. Billy watched Balthazar walk away. He waved to him one last time and began to look for someone to talk with about Jesus.

Billy saw a man sitting close to the temple with a jar next to him. A few coins were in the jar as Billy approached. Balthazar had given Billy some money earlier at the natural spring, and he thought it may be a way of beginning a conversation by donating some coinage to the man's coffer. Billy bent over and dropped a coin in his cup.

The man looked up at him and said, "Thank you for your kindness."

Billy asked, "Sir, was there a man here recently who is called Jesus? He would have come to the synagogue if he entered the city."

"You have missed the Son of God. Yes, he was near here, but he did not come in the city. Many talk about him. Those who meet him are changed. I myself was hoping he would come in the city and help me. You see, I am crippled, paralyzed, and unable to walk. Perhaps he will travel this way again?" asked the man after repositioning himself with his hands on the ground.

"I am very sorry you were unable to meet him. I recently met a man named John the Baptist who was very helpful to me. He is the one who suggested I follow Jesus and try to meet him," said Billy as he put another coin in the paralyzed man's cup.

Just then a very strong wind rolled through the streets of the city. It was a strange wind, as it howled more like an animal than an act of weather. The paralyzed man put a shawl-like garment over his head as it passed, using it as a hood. The wind left as quickly as it came and with less noise as it swirled up dust and other debris before exiting the corridor of streets that led to the temple.

"My brother, John the Baptist has been telling of Jesus's coming. I have never met his acquaintance, but I have heard a lot about him. One can learn a lot by sitting quietly here next to the temple. It has stirred up a lot of controversy in Capernaum and has drawn some looking for Jesus and more for John. Some of those looking for Jesus and John do not have good intentions. Be careful. I have heard Jesus is now potentially on his way to Cana," said the man.

"Thank you for your time and conversation. I pray you, too, will have the opportunity to see and meet Jesus. We both have the same quest, though mine will continue to Cana. I fear both of us will have to be patient as the opportunity reveals itself," said Billy.

Both men said farewell, and Billy headed toward the Sea of Galilee. He did not want to waste any time if Jesus was not in the city. If Balthazar had found similar intelligence, he would be waiting for him at the well he described. Billy was stopped in his tracks by a terrible feeling, however. He felt the hairs on his neck stand up and he quickly developed a sour stomach that made him cough and almost vomit. Drawn back in the direction of the synagogue, Billy was compelled to turn and there he saw it.

He turned around and saw this thing. It was a creature and there were people moving busily on their daily tasks and business on all sides of him. The creature Billy beheld was different than all of them. The people moving around it were covered in clothes of different colors and their faces were flush and full of life. The creature, who Billy noticed was intensely looking at him, was gray and lifeless. Its eyes were no vibrant color and blacker than anything. They were evil eyes and they were looking at him.

The creature was on a set of stairs that led downward to the synagogue. With strange, spastic motions that were jerky and inconsistent, as if it were fighting with itself, the creature approached Billy. Billy was momentarily frozen and now it was heading toward him. Billy looked where the paralyzed man had been and realized he was gone mysteriously.

No one knew him there and he was impotent to cry for help. The creature was a human, but something was very wrong. Why did it look like a charcoal drawing and what happened to its eyes? When it drew close to Billy, there was a smell of sulfur and wood fire as if someone was burning brush and leaves in autumn.

"I know who you are Billy. You do not belong here. There are many like me here among these people looking to do the will of our master," said the creature as its mouth moved, but it did not match the words coming out.

"Are you looking for Jesus too? Is he your master?"

"No. My master is more powerful than God or Jesus or your unfortunate John the Baptist," it said while it twitched its neck and looked visibly uncomfortable.

"Who or what is more powerful than God?

"You know of whom I speak," the creature stated as it looked at the synagogue and shuddered.

"What is your name, demon?" Billy said, thinking the only thing this foul creature could be was dark.

"We are many, and we serve the dark one. Our master wants you to join us. He wants us to tell you that it is folly to chase after Jesus. He does not want to meet and speak with you. If he really cared, he would have saved your father," said the evil creature.

Billy was in shock. So many strange things had happened to him in such a short time. How did this thing know of his father? It struck him in the heart as Billy had asked that same question many times in his private thoughts after his father's death. Why did God or Jesus take his father? Just then he felt strong and powerful hands on his shoulders. Balthazar found out Jesus was not in the city, too, and quickly had come looking for Billy rather than wait at the well so they could continue their journey.

Balthazar said something that Billy did not understand for the first time since the baptism. It seemed like an old language that was difficult to say. The words that came from Balthazar had a crushing effect on the creature, and for a moment the body and face of a young man were uncloaked from the oppression of the demon. A young man was beneath the evil charcoaled veil of evil.

The young man, unencumbered by the foul spirit, said, "Help me."

Just as quickly as the young man returned to his body and life flushed into him, the dark gray evil spread back into his body, and the same dark eyes and expressions returned to the body. It crouched into a powerful position, like a weight lifter poised to spring, as if it were going to strike out.

"You have no power here, magi's apprentice," shrieked the creature in a shrill voice.

Balthazar again recited the indescribable words from before and the creature cowered and retreated slightly. Balthazar said them again more emphatically. The creature stumbled and crossed the courtyard in front of the synagogue as if the young man was fighting the evil, scrambled up the stairs from where it came, and could not be seen any longer.

CHAPTER 6

CANA WINE

Billy and Balthazar moved south from the synagogue and away from their newly found adversary. When they made it out of the city and confirmed that the creature was not following them, they stopped to gather their thoughts. Though the creature was moving away from them when they left, they were obviously afraid of its deception. The creature was pure evil. Billy was visibly distraught. A demon had just confronted him in front of the synagogue.

A leopard, biblical figures, and now a demon were in this time and place, and Billy had been involved with all of them. For the first time in a while, Billy felt the despair he had as a child after his father's death, which carried into his adult life. The fear was that there was nothing stopping bad things from happening, and there was nothing he could do about it. Billy could do nothing about his father's death. It simply happened, leaving an enormous hole in his life. His grief then toppled his spirituality and then eventually his physical world.

It led him to be the man on the couch. If he didn't care about anything, nothing would hurt him if it went sour. It was a perfect defense. The evil of the creature brought back feelings of despair. Such was the power of this darkness. Perhaps because they were in biblical times and not in the modern world the reality of the demon was even more terrifying. Billy lived where science and logic had eliminated all superstition and wonder.

"What just happened? What were those words you recited? It seemed to be affected by the words and by you," said Billy.

"You know I am the son and grandson of a magi? I come from learned people. Part of the magi mystique translates into a magician or even a sorcerer. I have been trained to deal with his kind. Long ago, our people were much more involved with the world of good versus evil. Very few of us still know the words and incantations that help thwart or disengage a demon from its captive. Remember, there was a human in that body. The demon is an unwanted guest. Really, I should not say the word *guest*. The demon is not of this world. They usually appear when Lucifer wants to interfere with the natural world and its people that God created. I can't help but think your presence prompted the demon's visit."

"Me?" Billy said with fear and frustration. "How does the devil know I am here, and why does he want to stop me from meeting Jesus?"

"Every battle, great or small, for the soul of humanity is important to the devil and his demons. He must not allow you to meet with Jesus. There is some greater good that will come from your opportunity to speak with the Son of God. Maybe the encounter will affect hundreds or thousands. Then again, it may only affect you, but regardless of how many it affects, it means that good wins and evil fails. Each and every battle is important, Billy."

The two travelers decided to put some distance between themselves and the creature they encountered in Capernaum. They headed west based on the information Billy received from the paralytic man. Billy told Balthazar about the poor man crippled at the synagogue and how he was a person of many qualities. Billy told Balthazar that he hoped Jesus would return to Capernaum and bless both the crippled man and the demon-possessed young man, freeing both of them of their afflictions. Billy did not catch the name of the paralyzed man and hoped to do so upon another encounter, if given the chance.

"Keep the incident of the creature and discussion of it to a minimum. Speaking and thinking about it will give it more power and enable it to seek us out. Let us speak on it no longer," said Balthazar sternly.

The sun began to set, and they needed to rest and eat. They chose a safe ridge above the road. For anyone or anything to get to them, it would have to come up a steep area with loose rocks on all sides. It would be easy to hear anyone coming, and it would be difficult to move quickly up the rocks. Balthazar explained the strength of their position, which gave Billy some comfort as they prepared their food by the fire. Balthazar's sense of humor returned, and he mocked Billy, as Billy's head would snap in the direction of any movement or sounds.

"It is good to be on guard, but we have a good position. We will hear anyone coming our way, and the position itself will stop most who may want to do harm to us from trying to close the distance up hill on loose stones," Balthazar said.

"Forgive me, Balthazar, if I am on edge after all I have experienced and after what happened today. I appreciate you laughing at me, however," Billy said sarcastically.

Getting some warm food in their stomachs, tasting the sweet grapes from the secret vineyard, and drinking the refreshing water from the natural spring raised their spirits and allowed them to appreciate the positive experiences. Retrieving the water and the grapes that day were certainly a wonderful thing. Regardless of what happened with the evil creature, they had a lot of more positive things to enjoy than negative things to overthink.

The two travelers cleaned up after supper, prepared for bed, and tried not to dwell on the demon. Balthazar fell asleep almost immediately. Perhaps he had more faith than Billy. Billy struggled to fall asleep, tossing in his blankets and sitting up when he heard any sound all night. He thought that if his day had been different he probably would not be so jumpy and would have fallen asleep as fast as Balthazar. Billy tried a trick he had used as a child after his father's death. He would allow his mind to slow down, thinking about something positive that made him happy.

When he was a boy, that would have been memories of his father, special games, or events that made him remember how things were before his father died. He thought about his wife and children. Without pressing, he thought about their faces, trying to remember the small details. He dreamed of hugging them and kissing their faces. He imagined the happiness of one of the kid's weddings and the possibility of grandchildren. Amid his thoughts and dreams, Billy was able to fall asleep. The next morning, they were headed to Cana and hopefully one step closer to Jesus.

Billy woke up before Balthazar. The sun was threatening to come up but had not yet risen. The fire that had kept them warm through the night was no longer active. Billy heard feet on the loose rocks faintly. The footsteps seemed to be going around the ridge. He could not make out who or what it was, but it was moving quickly and irregularly. It sounded like something that could not make up its mind.

Billy called to Balthazar, who was in a deep sleep. "Balthazar, Balthazar wake up!"

"What is it?" exclaimed Balthazar, startled as he was awakened.

Balthazar quickly remembered the events from the day before. He remembered the frightening events after being asleep through the night. Both men were now standing and following the footsteps as they made their way around the foot of the ridge below. Balthazar was right. This position was difficult to mount and was even more difficult to do so without making a lot of noise.

Balthazar ran to draw his sword from its scabbard, while Billy followed the wayward footsteps. The sun was beginning to rise in the east. They would soon be able to see what was painstakingly walking around for an access to the top of the ridge. With his sword in hand, Balthazar got closer to the edge of the ridge to see their antagonist.

There, looking straight up at him, was the creature from Capernaum. It had tracked them there because of their original loose talk and thoughts about it. One could not blame the two for having those thoughts. Nevertheless, there it was, looking up at the top of the ridge, looking up at Balthazar. The evil being shouted angry profanities at Balthazar.

Balthazar fell to his knees, and with great feeling he recited the words he had used earlier to drive away the demon. Loudly concentrating on every word of the old text, he attacked the demon with his words. The old magi incantation was successful. The creature, in agony from the words, turned back toward Capernaum and ran from the ridge.

Because of the position of the camp, both men were able to see the creature still moving toward the city and felt the safety of the distance between them and the demon. They ate breakfast, watching the small dust kick up from the being as it returned to the city. They were now safe to make their way to Cana.

For part of the journey to Cana, they hugged the northern part of the Sea of Galilee until they needed to head more southeast, passing just away from the sea. The terrain grew more rugged as they moved away from Capernaum and the sea. Billy swore the geography of the area was nearly identical to the wilderness he originally traveled through. There were large outcrops of rocks, sparse vegetation, and coarse, small rocks and gravel at their feet.

Billy kept his eyes open for snakes and larger animals. They did not encounter any snakes and luckily no leopards. Billy thought the leopard was most likely only there because it had a job to do. It was to push him to the river and John the Baptist. When the leopard had pushed him, he did not know where he was headed, where he was, or what period he was in. Now he and Balthazar knew where they were going and had a plan. No need for a big cat to guide them or scare them to where God wanted him to be. The confidence of this knowledge was reassuring.

The two men were happy to have risen early to get a jump on

the day, but unhappy they were awakened in such a manner. Both men were tired as they progressed toward Cana. They were making good time in the cool air of the early morning. If they pushed hard, they would make it to Cana just past midday.

They both conversed as they walked about how they would go about finding Jesus. Both men agreed they should split up to be more efficient, as they had done in Capernaum. Balthazar could sense Billy was uneasy about being alone and away from Balthazar.

As they reached the outskirts of Cana, Balthazar took a minute to talk to Billy. He wanted to reassure him and to give him faith so he would not be afraid of any other demon creatures he might encounter. Balthazar told Billy that he was unable to teach him the old words that would repel the creature or others like it. Only the magi were allowed the knowledge of the old writings and teachings.

Balthazar reached into one of his travel bags and revealed an object on a medium chain that looked to be light in his hand and would reach the top of a man's chest if worn around the neck. The object was something Billy had never seen before. It looked to be something exotic and otherworldly.

"This talisman has been in my family for years. Only a magi can give this object as protection. It belonged to my son. I now give it to you for your protection while you are separated from me."

"I thank you, Balthazar. How do I use it?"

"If you see another creature, or possibly the same one we have seen, take the talisman with your hand and raise it in the direction of the creature. It will be repelled."

The two men then entered the city of Cana together and separated to find Jesus Christ. Balthazar was to cover the eastern part of town, and Billy was to examine the western part. They were to meet in the afternoon after their investigations concluded or if they heard of where Jesus was or if they directly encountered him. Both wished the other good luck, and they set off on their quest to find Jesus.

Balthazar found a temple on the eastern part of the city. As before, he looked to speak with someone who looked to be less important and who did not mind sharing information but would also keep to themselves so that the authorities were not informed of any inquiries being made regarding a prophet said to be the Son of God. Balthazar spoke to several good candidates.

Two of the men he spoke with had never heard of Jesus. A woman he spoke to had heard stories of Jesus and John the Baptist, but she had not heard that Jesus was in Cana or anywhere near the city. Finally, Balthazar spoke with a man who had just finished giving a sacrifice of a dove in the temple. He had just seen Jesus the night before in Cana.

Jesus was at a wedding the man attended. The man mentioned that Jesus had provided the wine at the event. Balthazar thought nothing of the man's remark about the wine, but he thought it was very generous of Jesus to offer the wine at a wedding in which he was a guest.

Across town, Billy was having even better luck. There was a large group of men mostly seated in front of what seemed to be a place to eat. He was hoping one of them would have come across Jesus or heard of his whereabouts. All the men looked to be plainly dressed, except one, who was dressed much more lavishly. He approached them at a steady pace, hoping to engage them quickly and extract any information available. The men seemed quite content and received him and his questions well.

"Good afternoon, gentlemen. I pray you are having a great day," said Billy, trying to get on the good side of this group.

"Of course! Absolutely. We are enjoying this day after such an incredible night," many of them said together. The group shared a jovial disposition.

"I am glad you are having such a good day," Billy said, preparing to ask the men about Jesus and his whereabouts. "Wait, you said last night was incredible. What happened to make it so incredible?"

One of the younger men stood up. His youth was his only distinguishing feature. The other men had variations of beards and facial hair, but the man who stood up had rosy cheeks and was not yet able to grow hair on his face.

The young man started his discourse like a sports reporter covering the big game. He said the men that were before Billy were at a wedding the night before. The bride and groom were not rich. The wedding reception began in a lackluster fashion. The wine served was not particularly good. Normally, a wedding party starts with the best wine and moves to weaker wine as the party progresses. The men noted that with such a poor selection of wine to start with, there was concern the party would fizzle quickly.

Then there was a rumor that the wine had run out. Not only had it been poor wine to begin with but now there was no more wine to be served. Many of the men added to the younger man's story that they were preparing to leave the party and go home if they were going to keep serving such poor wine, or if the rumor that the wine had run out was true.

The young man continued saying that Jesus then walked into the reception with his mother and his disciples. Many at the party had heard of Jesus, and he created a buzz among the wedding party when he walked into the celebration. Jesus, his family, and his disciples were invited guests.

A man walked up to Mary, Jesus's mother, and whispered something in her ear, since he was embarrassed to say out loud what he was asking. Jesus was unaware of the conversation, as he was seated and was watching other guests enjoying themselves at the party. It was as if he had more important things on his mind as he looked upon the festivities.

Mary came over to Jesus with a serious look on her face. According to others who were listening, Jesus's mother told her son that the wedding party was out of wine. Jesus immediately laughed and told his mother he did not want to get involved. Jesus was not upset or being mean. He did not want to draw attention to himself and take it away from the celebration.

Feeling compelled by his mother's words, Jesus told the head servant to fill large jugs with water and bring them into the feast. He then instructed the servant to taste the water. The servant was shocked to find that the water was no longer water, but wine. According to the young man, not only was the water turned into wine but it was a much finer wine than the original wine they served. There was more than enough for all who were there for the rest of the night. The entire group reveled in Jesus's miracle and generosity. Jesus had saved the party.

All the men who were sitting there in front of the place where the reception was held were still inebriated or hungover from what they drank last night. Billy noticed some of them had not stopped drinking. They all spoke of Jesus with high praise.

It was unclear to Billy if the men were impressed by the miracle or more likely just happy because Jesus had provided them with exquisite wine and extended the length of the party. Billy laughed because this drunken lot was benefitting from Jesus's miracle. Jesus had made all these common men his fans by simply getting them drunk.

"Gentlemen, I am happy for you that Jesus was so gracious to you and the other guests. Do any of you know if he, too, is still here on the premises or in the city of Cana?" Billy asked.

One of the men who was drinking out of a large jar that looked more like a flower vase than a drinking vessel stated, "He left with his disciples and mother before the reception came to an end. It was heartbreaking to see him leave. Some of us urged him to stay in case we ran out of wine again. He, of course, smiled at our request to retain him. He quickly cured our worries and told us it would be a challenge to empty the jars he had blessed."

"You will not run out of wine tonight or tomorrow, for that matter," Jesus said and then left the party.

None of the men knew where Jesus went. They were grateful for his delicious wine, however. Billy also pressed them, asking if they had seen his disciples or his mother since last night. All of them responded with negative answers. Suddenly, Balthazar was behind him, placing his hands on Billy's shoulders.

"There was a wedding last night here in Cana, and Jesus was here last night and may still be here," said Balthazar as Billy turned to greet him happily.

"Balthazar, you are looking at a group who was at the wedding reception and was blessed to have witnessed Jesus take large jars of water and turn it into fine wine in front of them. Many of them are still enjoying the very same wine Jesus created. It is possible some of them may not have experienced any sleep last night, enjoying Jesus's miracle," said Billy, smiling.

"Is there any left?" Balthazar asked with his cheerful smile and hopeful expression.

Billy was impressed with Balthazar. In the short time he knew him, he realized he could be stoic and stern, but he was also very human. The young man showed Billy and Balthazar one of the large jars the men were drawing from. The young man extended his arm, offering Billy and Balthazar to join them and to partake in the wedding wine Jesus transformed. Having only enjoyed the refreshing water from the natural spring, Billy and Balthazar decided they would enjoy a celebratory glass of the wine that Jesus made for the party.

"One glass," said Billy.

"One glass," Balthazar agreed.

The two filled glasses given to them by the men with the special wine. They both raised their glasses to the group and then to each other. The wine was delicious. Jesus had truly performed something miraculous in Cana. The other men cheered as the two drank from the cups. This was a moment to be celebrated.

Pointing at the talisman around Billy's neck, one of the men asked, "Why are you wearing a child's toy around your neck?"

CHAPTER 7

FAITH AND TRUTH

"Balthazar," Billy said with a stern tone.

"It is not a talisman. It is not religious at all. As a matter of fact, it is one of my son's toys attached to a chain. I needed to calm your fear, Billy. We needed to find Jesus. Please do not be angry with me. I wear it to remind me of my son when I am away from him."

"You sent me into that city with that lunatic—that creature looming over us. I could have been attacked or killed," Billy said, clearly upset.

"I believe that creature and others like him will be after you and after us wherever we go. Talismans will be of no use to us, especially this one that has no religious meaning to the creature. Faith is what is needed. For whatever reason, you chose to believe in the talisman.

"Could it be that you want to believe in the power of God and the power of God's son born among us? You did not ask me what it was or what it meant religiously. It was false faith, as you now know, but it gave you confidence to go into the city.

"Again, I will apologize one last time for tricking you, but the faith or peace of mind you found from what you thought would protect you, we need to find in our minds and our hearts. We need faith. I have heard you speak about the faith you had as a child before the death of your father. You were confident in yourself, your belief, and the way your world worked. It made you a better person. When you lost your father, a part of that confidence and belief left you, and you wallowed in pity and doubt for a long time," said Balthazar.

"Stop it. Stop talking about my father and me. You don't know what happened or how difficult it was for me after his death. You weren't there," said Billy, showing his frustration and perhaps some guilt.

"I don't know the difficulty of losing a father? You seem to forget who I am and what I have been through. You act as if you are the only person in your time and in this one who has been through adversity. You need to decide what kind of friend you want me to be. If you want me to tell you what you want to hear rather than the truth, you need not travel with me. A true friend you can trust to tell you the truth or at times bend the truth slightly to help you. I may have lost your trust for a moment by giving you the false talisman, but right now and right here I need to tell you that your wasted years spent feeling sorry for yourself are behind you," said Balthazar.

"Again, I could have been hurt or worse. My frustration with my father's death is not unique, and I realize my difficulties as a child are not unique either."

"Billy, I am your friend. Please do not lose faith in me for this simple reason. We were brought together for a purpose. Clearly you can see that as you look at what we have both endured. Both of our fathers passed away when we were young. God blessed me with a strong grandparent who took me in and treated me like a son as I grew into a man. Perhaps I had an easier upbringing than you for that reason, but you need to look at some other factors.

"First, to be the paralytic man you spoke to at the synagogue. Can you imagine not having the basic functionality to walk where you wanted, to be unable to go to the bathroom without difficulty, or to be left to yourself while friends and family leave you alone because they don't have time or energy to carry you? Can you imagine what he is going through? Can you imagine what the young man is going through possessed by that creature? He is lacking control of his body. A demon has control of him. He is inside his own body, looking out and seeing the evil the creature spreads from inside his own shell!" Balthazar exclaimed.

"John the Baptist has been threatened by every government and religious leader in the region since he arrived to preach in the wilderness. Some say he knows when he will die. It will be violently at the hands of jealous imposters imposing their will on those they govern. He serves God by preaching and laying the foundation of what Jesus will bring to this world, knowing it may lead to his death. Many love him and follow him, but just as many others despise him. John has not known peace since he began to serve God in this way. He is both blessed and cursed. He is touched by God and knows much, but he is also aware that as Jesus walks among us, his time with us is limited, and his service will be done, yet he does not complain or mope in melancholy as you once did. He looks to God and says, 'How may I serve?'"

Billy could not look Balthazar in the face. Truth was a salty dish served with strong words, and he washed it down with the wine that Jesus had made from water. Billy turned to Balthazar and walked over to his new friend to offer something he had not wanted to give in earnest for many years. Without spilling a drop of the special wine, Billy raised his arms and opened them to Balthazar. He hugged his new friend deeply, and tears rolled down both cheeks unevenly. He quickly wiped the tears from sight, embarrassed, as he was among the regional men who were mostly open-mouthed after the strong conversation held in front of them between Billy and Balthazar. Balthazar stepped back from Billy with his free hand remaining on Billy's shoulder while the other still held his cup of wine at his side.

"The knot that binds friendship grows stronger and reinforced when we have these moments of faith and truth," said Balthazar.

"Please accept my apology for overreacting. I wasted many years without real feelings for my family and friends but mostly for myself.

I did not love myself, because I did not realize the love that so many had for me, wishing I was the man I had the potential to be. I know now what I was, unfortunately. But more importantly, I know now what I want to be. I have not known Jesus these many years. I did not seek him in my daily life, and I certainly did not celebrate him as a blessing or realize the blessings I had in my cup," Billy said, looking down at the empty wine glass.

He continued, "I felt your words deeply, Balthazar. Someone always has it worse than you. John the Baptist, the paralytic man, and even the boy afflicted by the demon are challenged in ways I could never imagine. For them, for my family, for you, and for me, let's find Jesus, and every time I regress and submit to fear or lose faith I pray my friend reminds me with the truth so I can see clearly. Finding the blessings I have rather than dwell on what I lost or don't have."

"It is my belief that the two of you need to seal your new covenant with another drink. Bring forth another glass for our new friends," said an older gentleman who was with the entourage of wedding goers enjoying the wine Jesus had blessed from water.

Balthazar and Billy looked at each other and then at the men who had been so gracious. Balthazar finished his glass with a final guzzle and took Billy's so that he could fill both of their cups. The men obliged them, filling the glasses to the top with the special wine. A cheer went up from all of them as Billy made a toast.

"May all of you be blessed. May all of us know true friendship like that which we just witnessed, especially when it is difficult, and may we be so lucky to meet with the Son of God who walks among us that we may each find our way in this world with God's blessing."

Balthazar smiled and turned his head slightly to acknowledge Billy's toast and blessings. It went without saying that Billy had just given a toast that was closer to a prayer. Balthazar knew that Billy probably hadn't spoken like that in public in a long time and that he barely prayed. Balthazar drew strength from Billy at that moment. His friend had grown with him. They were sharing Jesus's wine.

Together they would have a wonderful adventure finding the Son of God. They would be challenged by evil and the hardships of the journey.

They would be pushed by simple human needs and tugged at the sides of friendship on both their parts in that regard. But if the two of them emerged from these days stronger than they were right now, with a glass of blessed wine in their hands and simple joyous expressions, they would be better men. They would be better human beings.

The two decided they would help the men finish the wine, get something to eat, and continue their quest in the morning. The two travelers had encountered much already that day. Between them and the men they shared these happy moments with, it became clear that the positivity of Jesus Christ had hit the group like an ocean wave filled with love and gratitude.

Other than the small tussle between Billy and Balthazar, there wasn't a sour word spoken among the men that night. They all spoke of Jesus and his miracle. They all shared how impressed they were with the resolution between Billy and Balthazar. It was clear that the influence of Jesus was not just in the wine or the inebriation of the group. The true miracle and power of Jesus could now be seen in the faces of the men and the joy surrounding all of them as they drank and spoke. The true effect would also be seen in the men who were there witnessing a miracle and benefitting from it, as they soon were going to their homes and communities.

One person can change many lives. Billy and Balthazar were both great examples. Billy, though briefly touched by his father's love, found the love and confidence that only a son or daughter could gain from experiencing such mentoring. He had an imprint from his father that could not be wiped away by the bearing of his father's untimely death. Balthazar was mentored by his grandfather—a man who already witnessed the power of God and the majesty of Jesus when he visited Mary and Joseph so many years ago when he and his learned friends crossed miles and miles to see the Son of God.

Balthazar was a true friend. He was a true friend because he was brought up by his strong father until his death and then his amazing grandfather afterward. When one positively mentors a child, influences another life, or gives stern truth to a friend, the world is a better place. The world was better for having Balthazar, his father, and grandfather.

It would now have another human being who can influence those around him. Billy was now a part of the ranks of doers and changers energized by the help of others that will influence the small part of the world they live in, whether in biblical times or his own. Billy was becoming an instrument of movement and change.

The men shared kind words and stories into the darkness of the evening. Billy and Balthazar were offered numerous places to spend the night. No one would be slighted from hospitality, as Jesus's wonder and blessings resonated among them. All who were there were changed from the presence of Jesus and his miracle, charged with energy from his divinity.

Several men commented that they wished to be as helpful as Jesus. They said these things knowing they could not turn water into wine as he did, but with their own talents could assist and accomplish much. Again, there was power in an act of kindness—an attempt to help one's fellow human beings, making their time on this earth easier. Jesus's actions supplied further fuel for Billy and Balthazar to complete their goal of meeting him. Regardless of the challenges their path may take, they were invigorated with positive energy and a desire to do good in the world. That was the power of the Son of God flowing through them.

The wine was still abundant, and the men were determined to finish it. They shared the copious amounts for hours. Some of the men went to the establishment for food. The innkeeper was more than happy to provide them with sustenance. The men ate together there, where Jesus had turned water into wine. Billy and Balthazar were offered several places to stay that evening, but the one man who was dressed extravagantly insisted the men come home with him. He introduced himself as Rufus.

Even though the men had too much to drink, they were not volatile or disrespectful. Seeing that Rufus was unyielding about Billy and Balthazar staying with him, the other men acknowledged he would be the best host for the two. Rufus was a religious man but also very wealthy.

Rufus was a middle-aged man from Nazareth originally. He had long, thick red hair and was more Roman than Jewish. Rufus did not look like the other men still at the party. He was slightly overweight, and his face was full. His clothing was more ceremonial than the others and contained gold thread, which seemed quite lavish, considering what the other men wore at the event.

He grew up poor, as most people did in those times, but came to work for a wealthy landowner near Cana in his formative years. The landowner he worked for lost both a son and a daughter to the same sickness when they were young. Rufus showed great promise and initiative and was rewarded by the landowner by being adopted as a son. When the landowner passed away, Rufus inherited all of the man's land, livestock, and belongings. He was a self-made man, noticed by a wealthy landowner for his hard work who believed in God and now his son, Jesus.

Rufus's home was just southwest of Cana and a short walk away. The three men may have taken longer to arrive due to their drunken state. The estate was impressive. An energetic servant greeted them when they arrived. Rufus suggested they eat again. The servant prepared a delightful spread of meats and cheese, with exotic fruits and figs.

Rufus had an amazing home with five sleeping quarters, including his own. He was a bachelor living with his servants. Rufus enjoyed the comforts of his abode, but he really loved working the land he had inherited and honoring his benefactor by succeeding with his endeavors and sharing with others. Rufus was invited to most weddings and celebrations in the area because he was loved and respected. Billy and Balthazar were impressed.

As they entered the structure, they noticed ornamented art and vases in a sitting room and a large dining hall where they ate. There was another room off to the northern part of the estate, where they assumed the kitchen and servants' quarters were located, as the main servant returned with refilled plates and cups from that area.

Both men were full and ready for a good sleep. Rufus and the servant led the men out of the dining hall back into the sitting room, which was adjacent to a lovely courtyard filled with trees and shrubs and more sculpted art. Looking upward, Billy and Balthazar saw the immense complexity of the home as stairs led up to a master bedroom for Rufus and onto a tremendous mezzanine overlooking the courtyard and the entrance to the house. The servant showed them both to their own separate rooms, which were on ground level. They were truly being spoiled. Rufus bid them a good night, and the three men went to enjoy their slumber.

CHAPTER 8

WISDOM

The latticed windows inside the room allowed for warm sunlight to penetrate the space Billy occupied for the night and made funny marks of checkered daylight on the bed where he awoke. The day brought vision, and Billy saw the fine decor of the room—lavish for a guest room. He rose slowly, feeling the pain of too many cups of wine, as if the large vats from which they refilled their cups were full and pressed on top of his forehead while he slept. It had been a long time since Billy experienced a hangover. Though he was miserable and gloomy back in his own time, he did not give in to drinking alcohol or other vices. He simply laid around a lot and watched television, which became an addiction in itself over time. He became a lump on a couch, where he grew roots.

Billy would sometimes use the fact that he did not drink in his own defense, at the rare times when Sarah would complain about his lack of energy or interest in her and the children. He would mount the defense that he drank sparingly and would never hurt her or the kids. He just needed time to himself to calm his thoughts as he watched television. It wasn't as if he needed to remark about hurting Sarah or the children. This defense was poorly executed and rarely taken seriously. If anything, it lessened his credibility in the sense that she loved him regardless of his flaws.

As Billy shook off the sluggishness brought on by the alcohol, he was reminded of the feeling of a hangover, though he had experienced it infrequently during his life. He recalled the time he went to a family Christmas Eve party when he and Sarah were first married. Everyone at the party was having a good time. It was a rare occasion in which he was unfettered with the chains of what happened to his father. He was conscious of the moment and surrounded by his family and friends.

The mood of the party was joyous but changed when his mother arrived and began to ask him and Sarah about having their own children, the job he had chosen, and why he wasn't going to church regularly. She hounded him about being more energetic in front of the family, getting involved with friends, and being more active in the community. In short, she was pointing out all the things Billy did not want to think about at a moment in which he was enjoying life at a party.

When he overheard Sarah's mother talking with Sarah and her sister Marjory about children, he started to panic even more. It was almost as if he felt betrayed. He had lowered his guard briefly at the party to enjoy the festivities, but his mother and the others reminded him of the reality he was accustomed to. There was a large bowl of eggnog in the dining room. No one else had noticed it. Billy had one glass after another until he finished the entire bowl. It was loaded and laced with strong Brandy. He felt like he could not breathe and was being cornered by his mother and did not want the same from Sarah's mother. He had too much eggnog. He felt full. He was drunk.

Billy woke up the next morning on his couch. He did not remember how he got there. Sarah must have helped him to the car and into the house. His head currently felt like it did that morning. Sarah asked him what made him drink so much, and she questioned why it was eggnog he decided to overindulge on, as she told him he threw it up all over their car on the way home. She spent all Christmas morning cleaning up his disgusting mess. Billy was hungover that morning, and the shame of throwing up and his wife cleaning it up for him were equally as painful as the hangover that afflicted him.

He wished he could go back to that morning and hug her and give a heartfelt apology. He could not remember doing so. He wished he could go back to that Christmas Eve and tell his mother to mind her own business so he could go back to enjoying the party. He wished he never drank the eggnog, and now he wished he had less of the miraculous wine.

He stumbled from his room and into the bright courtyard. His friend Balthazar was already up and sitting at a small table, drinking something that steamed out of a cup. Rufus's servant Micah, whom they met the night before, had brewed a tea from wormwood, mint, anise, saffron, and hyssop. Balthazar looked up and noticed Billy.

"Ah, my friend, you are awake. Come and join me," said Balthazar, eager to talk with Billy.

"Not so loud, please," Billy said as he held his right hand to his head.

"My friend, if you are to hoot with the owls at night, you must recover and soar with the hawk by day," said Balthazar.

"I will not be hooting or doing soaring of any kind today."

The two men laughed. Balthazar mentioned that he felt the same way, too, but Micah had mixed the concoction he was drinking, and it was helping him with recovery.

"Micah, can you make another one of these drinks for Billy?"

Billy did not notice Micah standing off to the side of where Balthazar was seated. Micah quickly scurried off, leaving the two men, and went through the sitting room into the kitchen. He emerged excited from the kitchen shortly thereafter, carefully carrying a cup of his wonder potion and a pitcher with more, in case the men needed refills.

Micah was a true servant and friend to Rufus. He went about

his work as if each action reflected on he and his master. He wanted nothing more than to serve Rufus well. Micah wore a maroon robe-like outfit that covered a long beige undershirt. He had sandals similar to the kind Billy was wearing. A leather belt held his robe and undershirt together that revealed he was a slight man in contrast to his master Rufus. As Micah brought out some light food for the two men to eat, Balthazar asked Micah some questions to reveal more about himself.

Micah was from a small town called Jotapata just northeast of Cana. His family had been sold to the previous owner of the estate when he was very young. They had a hard life prior to working there. Born into servitude, his father was a hardworking man with very little. His mother wept often, but tried not to in front of the family. She missed the family they left behind, though their prior masters did not treat them unfairly.

He had one brother and no sisters. His brother, Jokim, was given a choice, and so was Micah, to stay when Rufus took over the estate or leave with no obligations to Rufus. Rufus wanted his workers to make their own choices and respected Jokim's desire to leave and live his own life in the world. Rufus also respected Micah's decision to stay and rewarded his loyalty and hard work. Rufus was a good master, and both Billy and Balthazar gained more respect for him.

"Micah, do you know of Jesus?" Balthazar asked as Micah refilled his cup.

"I should say I do. My master has talked about him. He is said to be the Son of God."

"So you are a believer, then, in Yahweh and his son on earth?" Balthazar asked.

"My faith is strong. We have waited for the Messiah for quite a while. It makes sense to me that God has sent him during these particular times. Our leaders in the church, our appointed rulers, and the Roman Empire have brought a lot of difficulties down on those they are supposed to serve and govern. I pray his presence will bring clarity to our times," Micah said as an informed and knowledgeable man rather than an ignorant servant.

"We are on a quest to find Jesus. We were too late to meet him at the wedding your master attended. That is where we met Rufus. He was still enjoying wine that Jesus had turned from water. He graciously invited us here after we all had enjoyed the remaining quantities left over. We want to get back on Jesus' trail. Have you heard where he might have gone following the wedding?" Billy asked.

As Micah thought about the question he was asked, Rufus emerged from the large sitting room into the courtyard. He stopped momentarily to look up at the sky and the new day and then proceeded toward the men. He was greeted by Micah, who immediately went to get him a glass of his brewed concoction and more food and refreshment from the kitchen.

"We were hoping Micah could reveal anything he heard about the movements of Jesus, but now that you are here we will ask you if you have any similar information," Balthazar asked the prominent landowner.

"Unfortunately, I did not hear where he and his people were off to next, but I have been thinking about your mission since we met last night, and you divulged your desire to meet the Son of God. I pray you will indulge me, new friends. I am an old man, and as you know, old men are prone to eccentricity. I am no exception to this common assumption." Rufus laughed after speaking.

"I feel your expedition is one of high importance, and you are truly dedicated to its task. Hearing of your troubles with the creature you encountered and other minor setbacks, I feel it my duty to pass upon to you wisdom in regard to your undertaking, if you will permit me this clemency," Rufus continued.

Both men looked at each other and said, "Yes."

"Any help or wisdom would be greatly appreciated," Balthazar said.

Billy stated, "You have been so gracious to us. Any help you can give us is welcomed."

"Well, as I said, I have given some thought to your circumstances. Though I am not a learned scholar, and I do not descend from the hereditary background and origins of the likes of your family, Balthazar, I am a man of faith. As you know, I am also a man of humble beginnings. Being a man blessed with years, I have seen much that allows me to comment to you now.

"None of us know where Jesus has gone. Your next steps are ambiguous. To give you any direction to begin would not be prudent, as it would clearly be conjecture and speculation. But I believe this is to be your path for a while. God has given you purpose and cause from the mouth of John the Baptist, but I do not think God meant for you to accomplish this task quickly or easily. There are some things to consider here," Rufus said.

"Your path may divulge new value and wisdom in various forms. Revelation. You may find yourselves learning new things as you journey. Hardship. You may find that hardship brings about continued determination and an appreciation for that which at times seems unattainable. Discipline. It is not enough to believe in God or his Son. You must discipline yourself to be devout followers. The new revelations, the hardships you endure, and the discipline it takes to follow this course may be what God intended you to endure and experience on the path to finding Jesus.

"You will need to gather information, develop, and execute plans and directions. You will potentially lose faith in the quest. No matter how weary of the task you become, continue. God spoke through John the Baptist to you, Billy. God directed you here through the blessing of your grandfather's wisdom, Balthazar. Were I younger, I would ask to go with you. Please take this last bit of information and do what you will with it.

"The two of you have been given a gift of friendship and purpose. In the end, you may receive more than friendship and purpose. Regardless, the two of you have been touched with God's hand. John the Baptist saw it in you, Billy, and the creatures you have encountered who have attached themselves to those poor souls also see it as well. Both good and evil are aware of your intentions. The two of you will experience both sides. I pray for your sake more good than evil. It is my opinion that you will need to travel to catch Jesus. In the end, though, the experience will be enriching, and you will need to part the wisdom of your findings with others. This is the blessing God has bestowed upon you, and you in turn will share this with others, helping those who will not have this opportunity to gain faith and wisdom through your findings and involvement. May your travels find you blessed. That is all I have to say."

Both Billy and Balthazar were shocked and amazed by the words of Rufus. Both men said nothing after he was finished speaking. It was not an awkward silence, however. The brief moment of quiet showed that there was contemplation to the words spoken.

Here was a man who barely knew them, but clearly listened intently the night before and with his wisdom predicted the future they may behold and prepped them for what they might expect. He had listened as the men spoke the night before as they shared the wine blessed by Jesus. The men could tell Rufus hardly slept the night before, pondering the words he would share with them that morning. His generosity and qualities were apparent. They both wished they could spend more time with him, but they needed to continue after Jesus.

As Rufus finished speaking, Micah returned from the kitchen. He handed a glass to Rufus and took some finished pieces from the table the men sat at. He stepped back from the table and spoke.

"In the kitchen, a cook who is also a new believer in Jesus told me something very interesting. He is confident Jesus and his group of followers are headed to Nazareth. Jesus is from Nazareth, and many have heard he will continue in that direction. Please forgive me if this information is incorrect, but hopefully it will give you a direction in which to begin."

Billy and Balthazar looked at Rufus, hoping he would indicate if he agreed with the new information presented to them. Both men believed Rufus was an intelligent man whose opinion could be trusted. Rufus was not long in their company, but he was clearly respected after he was so good to them and had issued thoughtful advice so eloquently.

Rufus paused, thinking, as the men looked at him. It was clear he was considering what the cook had told Micah. After a few seconds, Billy was just about to ask Rufus what his feelings were on the matter, when he simply nodded his head, showing he agreed with the information that was presented to them and that they should proceed toward Nazareth.

Nazareth was south of Cana and just north of the Esdraelon Valley. The Esdraelon Valley separated the regions of Galilee and Samaria and produced a majority of the wheat used in Jesus's time. Rufus explained he had lands in the valley, and his estate benefitted from the farming done there. The lands and estate he inherited were vast.

Rufus went on to say there were many places in that area where Jesus might be. He felt the men should travel first to Nazareth, as discussed, but also mentioned that many other towns, such as Sepphoris, Japha, Nain, Dabaritta, Tiberias, and Magdala, could be places Jesus would stop, as there were good roads connecting all of them. The agriculture of the area—the wheat he had mentioned as well as the vineyards, olives, and figs that covered the landscape—would help sustain a group of travelers. Billy looked to Balthazar as Rufus mentioned the various towns.

Balthazar had a good education on the geography of the area. It made sense to Rufus and Balthazar that Jesus and his group could easily travel through Galilee if his intentions were to preach and minister with good travel conditions. He reminded the two men that they should not be shocked to find out he had traveled back to Cana from those areas or traveled to Gennesaret, Capernaum, or Bethsaida, either by foot or by boat, as it was easily attainable. The sea made all things possible, as it provided food through fish to the entire region as much as the wheat and other products did, and it also provided transportation, allowing for the products of the area to be marketable and the souls of people to be reached.

At first both Billy and Balthazar were overwhelmed and somewhat disheartened by the way Rufus depicted the region. They both realized Jesus could be anywhere. Rufus saw the anxiety in their faces and reassured them that traveling to Nazareth would be a good start; however, they should always be open to finding information regardless of their plan. Rufus also was quick to remind the men that there would be those who did not appreciate the ministry of Jesus and his men. Some of them would be looking to do harm to Jesus and his followers, so they should be careful who they told their purpose and plan to, even though they would need to communicate with others for evidence of where the Son of God was located.

As they finished their breakfast and another glass of Micah's ancient hangover remedy, Rufus excused himself for a moment, got up, and spoke to Micah away from them. Any feelings of fear or trepidation about their next steps were eliminated by the dialogue regarding the region, since there was clear evidence Jesus and his men would most likely be in close proximity to Nazareth. It was his hometown, and the routes and available resources were abundant in that area. The Sea of Galilee also made the area a good choice because of its obvious immediacy.

Billy and Balthazar helped Micah take away the dishes. As Micah saw the two men doing his job, he insisted they stop and let him take care of the cleanup. Both men insisted right back that they wanted to help.

"We cannot have the grandson of a great magi cleaning up plates and cups. It is beneath you, my lord," said Micah as he continued, trying to stop the two from helping.

"And what about me, Micah? My father was not important. I should be allowed to help clean up and wash the dishes if I so wish," said Billy.

“Regardless of who you are, both of you are guests. Please do not dishonor me by doing what is mine to be done,” said Micah.

“Are we not friends now after this visit?” Balthazar asked. “I believe a friend may choose to help in any way he or she chooses. You did not have to ask the other workers where they thought Jesus would be traveling to, but you did. This is the act of a friend. Our actions are that of a friend. Please allow us to help, as we regard you as a friend.”

“I am truly humbled. Thank you to my two new friends,” said Micah.

After the men delivered the dishes to the servant’s area, they came back through the sitting room. Micah had organized their belongings and added supplies to their bags. It was all waiting for them before the entrance. As they thanked their host and new friends, they went out the front of the estate, and there were two donkeys loaded with more supplies and food for their journey. The value of friendship could not be more apparent to the two men as they left Rufus’s home. They were treated with such great accommodation and kindness that words could hardly describe the feelings they had in their hearts.

They all wished each other farewell, and the men began their journey to Nazareth.

CHAPTER 9

NAZARETH

The men set out with faith that the direction they were traveling was correct. They did not know if Jesus would be among the populace of Nazareth, but the idea that he should be in the region made for a good plan. The men did not ride on the donkeys, as they were loaded with the supplies Rufus had provided.

"I believe when Rufus took Micah aside at breakfast he must have told him to get us two donkeys and these provisions," said Billy, smiling at the thought of their new friends looking out for them.

"I believe you are correct, Billy. We will find it difficult to meet a better person on our travels than Rufus. The Lord is working through him. His qualities are apparent to anyone who meets him. Imagine that Rufus was once a servant like Micah. He inherited the entirety of that estate from those lowly beginnings. I believe that is why he treats Micah with such care. It was not long ago that he was no different than his servant.

"As Rufus does not have an heir, it is my prediction that he will award the estate to Micah. The beauty of the situation is that Micah does not serve Rufus because he believes he will ultimately be rewarded. He serves with love for his master, regardless of the possibility, because his master already treats him with love. Is this not what we have heard about the ministry of Jesus? Jesus tells all to love others as you would love yourself. I do not know about the future and your time, Billy, but it seems that in this time right now this teaching could not be needed more."

"In the time I come from, more selflessness and kindness are needed. I have seen more given in my short time here than in all my days on earth in my own time. Balthazar, I was part of the problem and never part of the solution. I am ashamed to say that Micah as a servant showed more care for us than I showed for my own family," Billy stated, looking morose, thinking of his lack of love and care shown to his kids and wife.

"Billy, I know you are angry with your past efforts, and clearly you failed those whom you love. Your challenge to change is increased by the fact that you are unable to reconcile with them while you are here. I have experienced your remorse through you and have seen the change this place and experience has had upon you. Stay strong as God continues to test your heart and mind. If there is fault left in you at the end of our travels, it is because you are a human being. The Billy of old does not live in your current heart and mind anymore. Feel brief sorrow for what you should have done in the past, but live for the chance to make amends."

The men traveled through Sepphoris on their way to Nazareth. Billy and Balthazar were impressed with the agricultural bounty and beauty of the region. It was a thriving area. Billy noted that the biblical accounts, movies, and references made by clergymen of his time in classes he attended did not depict what he was seeing. Billy went into more detail with Balthazar regarding the account of his grandfather and the other magi.

He explained how the story that was told made it seem like his grandfather and friends were traveling in desert sands during their trip. Balthazar confirmed that the magi would have encountered sand, as all sides of the fertile area they traveled in now were surrounded by desert in one way or another. The area was an active civilization of diverse geology, geography, and people.

Billy and Balthazar camped just south of Sepphoris that night. They had a late start that morning but did not regret the time spent with Rufus and Micah. Billy was reminded of how dark the area was at night. Away from the lights of the city in his own time, Billy looked up and appreciated the constellations. His father used to point out the beauty of the stars when they were together camping away from the light-polluted towns. Balthazar saw Billy looking up at them.

"My father and grandfather spent countless hours looking at the stars. They were very talented at identification. They have passed on much of their wisdom to me. I do not share their love of what the star is or where it is in the sky. I just love the stars for being stars. They are lovely and mysterious," said Balthazar.

"Did your grandfather ever talk about the star that brought them to Bethlehem? The star that led them to Jesus?"

"He did. He said it was the brightest star he had ever seen. It stood out so much that all the learned men of that age whom he spoke with regularly agreed it was a sign of the coming of the Son of God. There were numerous prophecies about his coming, but the star signified his arrival. To be truthful, the place where they saw baby Jesus is a mystery. At the time, King Herod found out that my grandfather and his two traveling companions had come to see the miracle of his birth. Sensing a plot and later having dreams and visions, as magi do, they never revealed the location of Jesus and his parents to King Herod. The star guided them to baby Jesus, however. As bright as any star that ever shined in the sky. Much brighter than any star the shines above us tonight."

"I can't imagine anyone from my time finding out that I am with you on a quest to find Jesus. It would be too much for some of them to comprehend. If I go back, how will I explain the events that have transpired? How am I to explain any of this?" Billy asked.

"Do not worry yourself over these things. Do not let your heart and soul be heavy with burden and concern. Remember Mary's plight. She was with child and without a husband. Joseph still loved her and did not question the ways of God. Noah was told to build an ark. He was told to gather animals in twos and prepare the ark for them and his family because there was to be a great flood. It would have been simple to question the ways of God for him, but he did not. If you get a chance to return to your time, simply tell them the truth," said Balthazar as he added more sticks to their fire.

The two men were enjoying delicious bread and honey that night, courtesy of their host from the last evening. They were also having a glass of wine from the supplies he provided. The wine was very good. It was not as good as the wine Jesus had made miraculously, but it was delicious nonetheless. Both men only had one cup that night.

Both were leery of too much wine from their previous experience, and without Micah there to make his incredible potion they were going to save their stores and get some sleep. Billy fed the donkeys given to them by Rufus with grain from Rufus's generosity while Balthazar collected more wood and placed it on the fire to last the night. The men said their prayers and went to sleep.

In the morning, they had more food from the supplies provided by Rufus, fed and watered the donkeys, then set out for Nazareth. They were not far from the city and made it there fairly quickly, traveling south. The road was well plotted and seamless. The two men also appreciated the donkeys, as they were loaded with all their belongings. Leading a few encumbered animals was a lot easier than carrying all the materials, water, food, bedding, and more themselves.

Upon entering the city, the men sensed a strange foreboding feeling that their day would be filled with challenges and perhaps some darkness. At the gates of the city, people did not greet them with friendly faces. Scowls and anger twisted the expressions of the inhabitants of Nazareth.

Something had recently happened there that the two were unaware of because its impression was still molded in the emotions of the people there. The deeper they went into town, more of the same. They led the donkeys close to the town synagogue. They paid the keeper of the stable for the storage of the animals and their supplies, unloaded, and set about looking for Jesus.

Outside the temple, several men could be heard talking about Jesus. Billy and Balthazar pretended to mind their own business and have a conversation of their own, but they intently listened to the conversations around them outside the temple.

Apparently, he had been in Nazareth the day before. He read from the scriptures and was well received as Joseph's son. He read from the book of Isaiah. They recognized Jesus from growing up in Nazareth. But then Jesus rolled up the scrolls of scripture, handed them back to the attendant, and began to speak his own words. Either he rebuked the town of Nazareth or remarked that they were not receiving him well.

It was unclear what exactly had happened, but like any rumor the town of Nazareth was upset with Jesus for some reason, and they were talking about it. One could not cross the courtyard in front of the synagogue without hearing the irritated words of the town's inhabitants. Jesus had done something. Trying to keep their anonymity, the two men shared with each other that it had to be some kind of misunderstanding. It sounded as if Jesus was well acknowledged when he immediately returned to his hometown, and then some action or words, most likely misconstrued, had led to the current mood and climate of Nazareth.

"Billy, I will listen to that large group of men speaking over there, and you to the large assembly in front of the temple. Between the two of us, we will find out if Jesus is still here or if this occurrence was enough to make him leave the city," Balthazar said. "Be careful what you say. This is growing into a mob scene. Anyone who opposes what they are saying about Jesus may be in serious peril."

Billy nodded and went toward the synagogue. Billy did not realize it, but he had all but assimilated in appearance to the people of the region. When he initially came to his senses in the Judean Desert, he did not have time to examine his dress and appearance, as he was pressed to move from the leopard. After he was baptized, wearing water-soaked sandals made him realize for sure that he was not back home. Like many of the things he experienced in this land, he accepted that he was dressed differently than he would be in his own time.

God had placed him there with the appropriate clothing and sandals to allow him to fit in. God awarded him the knowledge of the language so that he could communicate with the people he encountered. Billy accepted this as well. They were both blessings. At night, as the men laid down to sleep, Billy thanked God for these things.

He felt he had more time to contemplate this blessing. There were no cars, no cell phones, and no televisions. To travel somewhere, one must use their feet or animals. Certainly it decelerated the mind to not be wound up by electronics and machinery. It allowed Billy time to count his blessings both here and back home. He knew he was blessed. He was thankful he was blessed.

Balthazar looked across the courtyard in front of the synagogue and laughed. Billy had not shaved since he arrived. In the short time he was there, he had a full beard. For Balthazar, it took a few moments for him to pick Billy out of the crowd. Rufus had shared some extra clothing with the men and had Micah pack it into the supplies on the donkeys.

If Billy's wife and kids arrived at that moment, they, too, would most likely have a difficult time recognizing their husband and father, not only because he had a beard but because his body was different. His body language had changed, and more specifically he had lost fifteen pounds from traveling on his feet. In regard to his body language, it was unlike before because he stood taller and moved with confidence. Being in the presence of a strong male like Balthazar caused him to find his poise once again. He remembered standing next to Steven on a sports field and the time he was forced to defend the school playground in sixth grade.

A boy who was truant from his own school wandered on to the

school property, looking for trouble, and started pushing younger kids down, spitting on girls, and disrespecting the others who came to see what was happening. Steven, his friend, ran over to Billy, who was playing basketball with another group. Steven was late to recess and saw the ruckus as he made his way to the basketball court.

Billy turned to see the negative excitement, handed the basketball to the others, and confidently strutted over to the boy who was misbehaving. Billy recognized the boy. He was from a neighborhood close in proximity to where Billy lived. It was Lukie Lyman. Lukie went around the city selling illegal fireworks from sources unknown. He was known to be menace to all who crossed him and to some who just accidentally got in his way. Lukie was known to carry a knife that he was not shy about showing others.

Kids were afraid of him. Grown-ups were afraid of him. He was the kind of kid who grew up way too fast. He had a troubled upbringing that made him ornery, and he had a mustache that rivaled the famous front man of Queen, Freddie Mercury.

Lukie saw Billy coming. Billy was not notorious like Lukie but was well known in the city as a star athlete and as a stand-up guy. This incident happened right before the death of his father. Billy was at the height of his popularity and success.

"What do you want, dipshit? Is this your school? Must be—all the other losers are here too," Lukie said, standing over a younger and smaller kid he had just pushed to the ground.

Without hesitation, Billy walked up to Lukie, lowered his shoulder, made a fist, and punched him square in the nose. Lukie crumbled to the ground. Billy, remembering the knife, pounced on Lukie like a predatory animal, firing a barrage of punches to his face. Lukie reached inside his jean jacket to get his knife. Billy noticed his movements. Without missing an extra punch, he opened his palm and smacked Lukie's hand.

The knife came flying out of his jacket and across the parking lot. Lukie could do nothing but cover his face with his arms. Sensing the fight was over, Billy stopped his volley of punches. Blood covered

Lukie's face, mostly from his nose. Blood covered Billy's hands, mostly from Lukie's nose as well.

A teacher who was late for playground supervision came out to the carnal scene. He rushed to the battlefield, hoping to curb the attack, but it was already over. The small and younger kid who was saved by Billy's actions ran over to grab the knife and hid it behind his back. Lukie lay crying on the ground like a scared child, no longer a bully.

The teacher pulled Billy off Lukie and went to his aid. The teacher was about to lay into Billy but was stopped by the mass of children who simultaneously pleaded for their savior. The teacher took Lukie into the school for attention from the school nurse, and once he was situated the teacher returned to the playground. Children followed the teacher inside, making sure the truth about what had happened was told. As he approached Billy, his response to the situation was different than all expected. The teacher reached out and hugged Billy.

Putting his hands on Billy's shoulders he said, "You were a hero today, Billy. Not many young men would have the courage to stand up to that bully. What made you do it?"

Billy, who was still shaking from what had happened and was filled with enough adrenaline for a football team, looked up at the teacher and said, "I am not sure what happened. I saw Lukie pushing the kids, and I reacted. I really don't know why I did it other than this is our school and playground, and these are my friends. I wasn't going to let Lukie hurt them."

From that day, word spread throughout the city that Billy had beaten up Lukie Lyman. His status was forever secured in the myths and legends of the town. Steven came up to him and looked at his friend.

"Let's go wash you up."

Billy looked like a prizefighter who knocked out the champ without getting punched. He was shaken by the events, but he walked a little taller that day. It was that Billy, with a full beard, who stood tall among the crowd in Nazareth, seeking answers to the mystery of Jesus's fall from grace in his hometown, not the man who sidelined himself to a couch for many years.

Billy and Balthazar collected as much information as possible and returned to each other, meeting in the center of the courtyard.

"It sounds as if the trip to Nazareth was wasted. Jesus is no longer here," said Billy.

"My group said there were some things mentioned after he read the scripture in the synagogue. None of them knew exactly what was said, but whatever it was made those who were present angry, and then word spread throughout town quickly," Balthazar said, wiping sweat from his brow.

The sun was directly above them, marking midday. No clouds were in the sky, just a vicious sun pouring heat and light down on them. Billy was still trying to get used to the changes night and day produced in the region.

Speaking quietly so no one could hear his next words, Billy said, "The group over there stated that Jesus was escorted out of town. A few people wanted to throw him off a cliff, and others wanted to stone him. Balthazar, what do you think happened here that caused the people of Jesus's hometown to turn on him so quickly?"

Billy hadn't even finished his words when he saw it. It was standing amid the group of people where Balthazar was gathering information. It wasn't actively participating in the discussion but would whisper in the ear of another like it and then another.

This was a leader of the creatures. The evil spirits were at fault here. They were mixing in with the crowd and sparking hatred against Jesus. Billy pointed out the wicked being to Balthazar. It was a young little girl, but it stood as if a general. This poor little girl was seized by this spiteful malevolence that oozed assured wickedness.

The minions scurrying back and forth would change as they approached the small and large groups of people talking. One minute they would be gray and lifeless poor bodies getting orders from their leader, and the next moment they would infiltrate the people talking, turning themselves pink and fleshy with life again as to not be discovered. They spilled toxic words into the ears of the people there. This is why Jesus was now hated in his hometown of Nazareth. They spread like a disease over the crowd.

"Billy, I think we need to make haste from the city," said Balthazar as the scene grew chaotic and unruly.

The two men started to move away from the courtyard in front of the synagogue. The leader of the evil creatures stepped in their path every time they moved, like it was playing defense in a basketball game. The movements were not jerky like the other creature they encountered. This was a powerful demonic spirit, and it seemed as if it was sent to thwart their efforts specifically.

Balthazar grabbed Billy and turned around. He was quick to point out that Billy should not look at it or acknowledge it, as to not give it power. Billy looked back to see the evil thing laughing devilishly at its victory in Nazareth. The town was overrun with evil. Nazareth was lost. Billy began to feel sick to his stomach. He told Balthazar that he might throw up.

Taking the long way around neighborhoods while avoiding the creatures, the men made it to the northern gate of the city where they entered. Billy still had a sour stomach as they passed the gates. As they left the city, a feeling of relief overcame them. The tension created by the darkness was lifted from them, and Billy began to feel better.

Just then Billy realized something and said, "The donkeys and our provision are still in the stable!"

"Stay here," said Balthazar, sprinting back into the town.

Billy began to follow him but fell to the ground. The feeling of pain and discomfort overwhelmed him as he began to vomit violently. The evil was affecting his body. Moments later, as he composed himself, he raised up and stumbled toward the courtyard, where the livery held the donkeys, to assist Balthazar.

Balthazar emerged from the stable running, holding the leads to the animals, who were noticeably disturbed by what was happening. Two creatures followed him from where he came. They were chasing Balthazar. Lucky for him, the creatures were running out of control like the first creature they met. Sharp, jerky, and inefficient movements plagued their efforts as they tried to catch up.

Billy took one of the donkeys lead like a track star in a relay from his friend, and they expeditiously exited the city for the second time. They were far enough away from the city and could see they were no longer being followed, so they slowed down to calm the animals and catch their breath.

"When I arrived at the stable, the creatures were preparing to kill the donkeys," said Balthazar, out of breath. "I was only able to save some of our supplies. They were relentless."

"I am sorry I wasn't much help. I became very sick suddenly."

"The evil in that city is powerful. The spirit that inhabited the body of that poor girl emanated dark influence. It is of little wonder that Jesus was driven out. They knew he was coming. They knew we were coming, and they were ready to do battle. I have never experienced anything like that. I believe where there is great good there is also great evil. This happens not to create balance but because the battle between them is constantly raging. Like a commander, God and the devil send their troops to the conflict. We were beaten by numbers. I anticipate that Jesus will be challenged in his efforts and ministry as he travels these lands, but it was important to the enemy that he fail in Nazareth. To lose a foothold in one's hometown can be a challenging blow mentally and spiritually."

The two men were now heading east away from Nazareth. They traveled through the small town of Dabaritta and then turned north by the Sea of Galilee through Tiberias and Magdala. In Magdala, they heard Jesus was seen in Capernaum. Knowing the city well from their earlier travels, they headed that way.

The men camped miles from Capernaum one night. There was an unexpected storm, and the two were forced to find shelter. With no one else near to them and fires extinguished by the heavy rains, they were stranded and in trouble. Lightning and thunder crashed above and around them. The donkeys were frightened and took off into the darkness.

Alone, the two grabbed what provisions they could find in the darkness and ran toward a nearby cliff. Near the cliff was a hollow entrance. Without hesitation, the two climbed into it. Balthazar could be heard searching with his hands for something. Moments later Billy could hear rocks slapping together, and he could see small sparks shooting near the floor of their location. Balthazar was truly magical. He had started a flame from something dry he found in the supply bags.

They had been blessed to have so much for so long, relying on the provisions Rufus had provided. Now they were without the donkeys and had a smaller portion of what they had before. Balthazar struggled to keep his flame going. Billy looked in the cave for things to burn. Some branches, sticks, and sagebrush could be found, and he brought it to Balthazar. They grabbed and burned anything that wasn't wet.

Then the two heard a horrible sound. It sounded like wailing, but not from sadness. It sounded more like wailing from anger and despair. It came from the darkness of the back of the cave. The two men were startled. The sound intensified and grew closer. It was a singular sound. It was coming right for them. There was movement in the darkness.

A white, whispery, and long trail of mist was stirring, slithering left and right but not on the ground. As it drew near, one could see it had an eyeless face in the front and a disembodied tail trailing about ten feet. It sped up as it moved closer to the fire and shot up above them and clung to the side of the wall. It stopped howling and looked back at them and spoke.

"You two. You wretched creatures of God and followers of Jesus. I assume you have heard."

"We have heard nothing. What are you, foul soul?" Balthazar replied.

"I can't even hide from you in this cave without you disturbing my lament. I am the demon who possessed the boy. The one from Capernaum. The one who nearly attacked you at dawn on the ridge. Your Jesus saw fit to cast me out of the boy. The boy was my possession. Jesus won the fight over me, but I was told before that you and Jesus failed miserably in Nazareth," it said with a slithering tongue like a snake or lizard as it shook in anger on the wall of the cave.

"We do not fear you and will not suffer your torments," said Balthazar. "Be gone from our presence," Balthazar shot back, speaking the ancient texts against evil.

The demon turned a dark gray. It leaped from its position on the wall to the other side of the cave and then crashed down into the floor, only to rise up as if material and solid forms could be penetrated. It bounced like a pinball against the sides of the hollow walls, wailing and howling and speaking in strange voices and tongues, as it was visibly agitated by Balthazar's words. Then all at once it passed the two men and burst through the opening they had entered through, taking the light of the fire with it.

Balthazar quickly found the rock and flint, and he reproduced the flame, scavenging for the dry pieces they had gathered. A key battle was lost in Nazareth, but another was won by Jesus, driving out the unclean spirit from the boy. The boy was free from his tormentor. Jesus had won. The two, unsettled, would get little sleep that night.

CHAPTER 10

TRAVELS

The men were forced to remain in the cave for several days and nights as the rain continued. After what seemed to be a long while, light crept into the entrance of the cave where they had been camped for this period of time. They spent most of the first night looking to see if the demon would return. Billy was shaken by the presence of the evil spirit. It was one thing to see the creatures in the humans they inhabited, but to see it in its actual form and to hear its voice and cries was unforgettable.

The two had removed their clothes and hung them up by the fire, which they kept roaring day and night with any fuel supply they could find. The heat they experienced during the day was in sharp contrast to what they experienced by night. The days gave no respite, as the storm blocked the sun, and the rain lowered the temperature outside and then inside the cave.

They found much of their supplies gone with the donkeys or ruined by rain. At least their clothes were now dry, and they could put them on. The events from before weighed heavily on the two. They both agreed to gather what was usable and head out to look for the animals, in case they had returned when the weather finally permitted.

There were not only storm clouds outside but cloudy negative thoughts as the two sat isolated and frightened inside the cave. The trials in Nazareth followed by the encounter with the demon were morale killers. The darkness of the cave and the shadows from the fire on the walls added to the dark emotional climate. The two needed to get outside.

A break in the weather allowed the men their chance. Crawling out of the hole, their eyes were not adjusting well to the sunlight, which they had been missing for several days. But as they felt the sun on their faces with the warmth of its rays, the two perked up and embraced each other in celebration. The two friends had been through a lot. Together they searched for the donkeys, but to no avail. Next they were off to Capernaum. Fearing they had wasted too much time in the cave and would miss Jesus, they passed by a town where normally they would have stopped.

Talking to several travelers on the road, they found out that the storm they encountered was isolated to where they were. Other people from around the area stated that there was not a storm and looked at them like they were irrational when they brought it up. Realizing the storm was another strange occurrence to be added to their experiences, they did not bring it up to anyone else and would inquire about Jesus instead.

To almost all the people who heard about the storm that they encountered through conversation, they did not want to speak with them any further after hearing about the phantom storm. People of this time experienced or heard about the paranormal. Prophets had been in this region for hundreds of years, performing miracles and accomplishing incredible feats. And now Jesus was among them. The locals they spoke to understood peculiar events but were superstitious of them unless they had seen the events with their own eyes.

Billy was convinced the science and logic of his time ruined a lot of the mystique created by miracles. He even thought it closed the hearts of those who might in other circumstances believe. Nearly everyone Billy and Balthazar encountered in this time and place had faith in God and some in Jesus as word spread regarding him. But in Billy's time, science and logic had replaced God. People were no longer searching for the wonder of God or miracles. Billy wondered if the demons had something to do with the disillusionment of the people of his future world.

For a significant amount of time, Billy and Balthazar continued to trail Jesus. They went into Capernaum and found that Jesus had been there. They heard about the miracle of Jesus driving out the evil spirit that attacked them in the cave. This gave them some comfort to hear the story from other people. The goodness of Jesus was winning regardless of what happened in Nazareth.

From Capernaum as a home base, Jesus reached out through Galilee, ministering to the people. Several people they spoke with told them about what Jesus was saying when he preached. A woman with an excellent memory came to them, as she heard Billy and Balthazar were looking for the Son of God.

"Please let me talk to you, friends. I have heard you are looking for the chosen one named Jesus. My name is Deborah. When Jesus was before us, my spirit was lifted by his words. He said he was sent to proclaim freedom to us all and that he would be a light unto the world for those who were previously blind. He said he is here to preach the good news that we will all have the opportunity for deliverance and favor from God."

"We are grateful you have sought us out and have shared the words of the Son of God with us. Thank you. Do you know where we can find him now?" said Balthazar.

"It is very hard to say where he is presently. Jesus has several close followers now. They seem poised to travel all over the region, spreading the message of hope and love. He has performed so many miracles. Bless you both for your faith in him. Please stay and eat with us before you continue to search for him."

Billy and Balthazar were happy to accept her offer. They sat down to eat with Deborah and her family. She had three children—one boy and two girls. Her husband was not at home. He was working in the wheat fields near Nain. The men were very thankful for the hospitality. They found Jesus's location. There was a glistening of hope, love for others, and charity.

His message was of forgiveness and grace and those words penetrated the deepest darkness and raised people from common partakers in life into active participants looking to do good by others. Billy experienced his own personal change, and he still had not met or heard Jesus speak. The Son of God was among them, and his effect upon the masses was as positive as the leader of those creatures was negative in the town of Nazareth.

After they ate and thanked Deborah for her kindness, wishing her and her family well, they were open to which direction they would travel. The people they spoke to near Capernaum were unable to tell them where they thought Jesus would be traveling. His ministry was on the move.

At the eastern entrance to the city, they noticed there were a lot of travelers heading out onto the roads. One man was organizing his belongings on a camel. They went up to him, asking why so many were leaving Capernaum.

"There are many here who have heard of Jesus Christ, the Son of God on earth. He has been here in Capernaum and is said to be traveling around the southeast side of the Sea of Galilee. I, with many others, plan on traveling that route to meet him."

"Do you feel it smart to travel? Why would you not stay in Capernaum? Jesus has been here several times before. Wouldn't it be safe to say he will return?" asked Billy.

"For many of us who have waited for a true messiah, this is the opportunity we have been waiting for, and we would rather travel out to meet him than wait any longer."

Billy and Balthazar were faced with a quagmire of problems. They were unsure of where to go next. Some of the people in Capernaum did not know where Jesus went. Others in the town were sure of where he was going and were ready to go out after him based on the desire to find him and had faith in his location.

"I am concerned with the lack of concrete information regarding where Jesus is or has been. We really know nothing more than what we learned in the cave. A demon was driven from a boy here in Capernaum, but are Jesus and his group of followers planning on making this city their home? Is he using this place as the base by which he will strike out to minister around the sea and further south, or will he always be transitory?" questioned Balthazar.

Both men decided to pray on the matter. Billy allowed Balthazar to lead the prayer, not because he wasn't a leader. Billy had regained much of his swagger since coming to Israel. Instead, he was being polite. Who was Billy to recite a prayer in the presence of the grandson of a magi?

Balthazar prayed, "Our heavenly Father, we humbly thank you for the food and company of Deborah and her children. Please bless her and watch over her and her family as she awaits the return of her husband. Thank you for delivering us from the demon in the cave and calming the storm. Thank you for the blessing of friendship and kindness that we have received on our journey. We are without a direction as we search for your Son. We pray that you will lead us in the direction that you want us to go. Please protect us from harm in our travels and continue to bless us with good fortune as we begin our next steps in this journey. Amen."

Balthazar was taught to read the stars and practice the search for signs since he was a child by his father and grandfather. He was very truthful with Billy and told him that he did not have any answers regarding where they were to go next. Nighttime was almost upon them. They decided to camp outside the city on the southeastern side. Balthazar wanted to look for signs in the constellations at night. If he saw nothing that would help them, they were resolved to head south down the Sea of Galilee like many of the others.

Balthazar went to their travel bags. Much of what they had with them was lost when the donkeys fled, but Balthazar was hoping some of his instruments he brought along were still there. He brought along ancient wisdom in the form of an astrolabe used to measure distance between the stars and earth. He wanted to look for anomalies that may indicate a direction for them. He spent much of the night looking up to the heavens.

Initially, Billy was very interested in the device and what his friend was looking for. But the longer he spent looking up with his friend, the more tired he became. He asked if Balthazar would be upset if he closed his eyes for a bit, only to rejoin him later. Balthazar was preoccupied with his deliberations and gave his approval. Billy went to lay down by the fire, and Balthazar continued to look at the stars as he slept.

The next morning, Billy awoke to find Balthazar had not made a place to lie down that night. With persistent effort, Balthazar was searching for information, but to no avail. As Billy picked up his blankets, he looked for his friend. Shortly after Billy packed up, Balthazar appeared with some food for breakfast.

"I was unable to discern anything last night from the stars."

"Did you not sleep?

"I was so anxious to find a sign in the stars that the entire night passed by. My father and grandfather were the same way. They could look at the stars for hours. As I told you, they really loved astronomy. I never shared their love for it. I was just eager to find a direction for us."

Without a sign from the stars, the two ate their breakfast, picked up camp, and headed down the southeast side of the Sea of Galilee. They were still determined to find Jesus, but the strain of the trip was beginning to weigh on them physically. Each morning, they found it harder to rise.

Food was becoming scarce, as was assistance from others. They attempted to keep their spirits bright, though, as they traveled. Billy and Balthazar told each other jokes and stories to amuse each other and pass the time. They provided a brief break from any negativity they were harboring. They would find difficulty in doing so, however, as they continued their failures in finding Jesus.

They traveled many miles in search of him. From other people they learned that he had gathered others to be his closest disciples. They heard that Jesus single handedly calmed a storm that threatened his people on the Seas of Galilee. Countless tales were told about him healing sick people and helping paralyzed men and women to walk again.

Jesus was curing people of diseases as serious as leprosy. He continued to drive evil spirits from tormented people who were oppressed by the powers of darkness. Jesus was conquering the things of this world that brought death and despair, but Billy and Balthazar were always just behind him and his good works.

Their timing was always slightly off. They would enter a town only to find out Jesus had just been there. They would see a man or woman on the road who was helped by him or witnessed him heal or preach. The people they would come across were overjoyed by the works of Jesus and the words he spoke, but Billy and Balthazar were unable to connect with the Son of God.

Bad news reached the two men as they were looking for Jesus. Billy and Balthazar had traveled down the eastern side of the Sea of Galilee, south as far as the provinces of Decapolis and Perea, near where John the Baptist had baptized Jesus and Billy. As they headed back north, meaning to travel through Judea and Samaria on their way back to the western side of the Sea of Galilee, a man was telling a small group that John the Baptist had been executed by Herod Antipas.

The man said John the Baptist had been arrested and imprisoned by Herod Antipas for speaking out against him after he left his original wife and took his brother's wife as his own. He chose not to kill John at the time because too many people in the region loved him, and he feared the repercussion and anger of the people. Deep down, Herod Antipas also felt John might be a special prophet as well, even though he himself was not a religious man. Herod feared what John might do if the power of God were to actually work through him.

Sitting down on a large rock and tired from travel, Billy cupped his hands with his thumbs around the outside of his face around his temples to cover his eyes. He leaned his elbows on his knees and began to cry. The first person he met in a land that was originally strange to him was John the Baptist. He was saddened and angry at the same time.

John was a good man, and although they were following Jesus, they had heard as many glorious stories about John the Baptist throughout their travels as they did Jesus. John was a simple servant of God sent to proclaim the coming of Christ. He never wavered from his mission and ended up imprisoned and murdered for telling the truth. The truth was that Herod should not have married his brother's wife.

Balthazar came up to Billy and put his right hand on his left shoulder. Balthazar said nothing, and Billy did not move. It was natural for Billy to be emotional. A friend was murdered. Billy thought back to all the times when relatives, family friends, or their parents passed away. He would never go to the funerals. After his father's death, it was almost impossible for him to go. He regretted not attending.

He should have supported his friends and family through those difficult times. He was selfish to avoid the funerals. Now again he would not go to the funeral of John the Baptist, another friend. He had only briefly met him, but it felt like he knew him well from all the stories he had heard. Balthazar and Billy did not know if there would even be a funeral for John.

It would make sense for Herod to keep his death as quiet as possible considering John's popularity with the people and even if they had a funeral it would take them away from tracking Jesus and would perhaps arouse suspicion. Any friend of John the Baptist might be considered an enemy of the State. They would have to mourn for their friend on their own. That night, both men prayed upon his death, thanking God for sending someone like John into the world. Later they heard John's disciples were allowed to take his body and bury it in a tomb.

The men traveled up the western side of Galilee, stopping at the southern Galilean town of Sennabris at the southernmost tip of the Sea of Galilee. There they encountered fishermen who said Jesus was recently in Bethsaida, which was southeast of Capernaum. Jesus was preaching to a multitude of people that grew larger as the day progressed. When he was near finished, his disciples asked Jesus if they were to feed the people, since it was close to suppertime.

Jesus was confused about their interest in food, as he felt his words were more important to hear rather than eating. He realized, though, that those gathered had been there for a long time, and they were outside the city of Bethsaida. He told the disciples to gather what food they had, but there was not enough. Jesus took the little amount of food they gathered, blessed it, and it multiplied. The man said the food they had would feed Jesus and his men. After he had blessed it, it fed nearly five thousand people.

Billy and Balthazar were amazed at such a miracle. They hoped if Jesus was traveling further north they would catch him at Capernaum. If they were headed south, they would meet him on the road. The two felt good they had not committed to heading further north on the west side of the Sea of Galilee after hearing about Jesus at Bethsaida.

The news of Jesus's whereabouts was fresh, too, as the fishermen had just sailed across the sea to Sennabris. They wasted no time traveling to find him. Unfortunately for Billy and Balthazar, Jesus had traveled the opposite way, heading northwest around the sea toward Capernaum. The two planned to stay outside Bethsaida, as they were both exhausted and weary from travel. They had covered a lot of land and seen many things, but what started as a simple quest became more complicated and time consuming. They remembered the words of Rufus and others who told them to keep their faith, though it be tested. Their faith remained strong. They would need to draw strength as they proceeded.

CHAPTER 11

ON WATER

Billy and Balthazar were weary from travel. They slept very late to regain their energy. Their provisions were running low. As they traveled, the men were unable to catch any rabbits or fish lately, although they had found it easy to find their prey up until this point. Up until now, they had been able to scavenge for meat and vegetation to eat. The supplies from Rufus ran off with their donkeys. It seemed that lately they were very unlucky.

Before turning in the night before, the two feasted on a less than hearty meal of stale and moldy bread. The two looked at the bread and thought back to the time when they had the fresh grapes and were just starting their journey. They were fresh, the grapes were fresh, and their thoughts of finding Jesus were fresh. Now their spirits and their physical bodies were like the bread they had for dinner—stale and unsatisfying. They needed rest, even though the pursuit of Jesus was ongoing. The two needed a break from the toil of searching, especially with empty stomachs.

Billy and Balthazar made camp at the base of a rock escarpment. As the men slept at the base of a large outcropping of rocks, the sun began to poke over the top of the rocks. The rocks were casting a shadow and were blocking the heat of the sun, allowing the men to sleep longer. Balthazar was wise to choose this spot, knowing they would be out of the wind and elements within the rocks, but also the enormous rocks would give day cover, allowing them to sleep longer and not be interrupted by the bright rays earlier in the morning.

The two slept hard and deep. They needed the rest. While they slept, Billy had a dream. He was holding his breath under water. It seemed as if he had been holding his breath for a very long time. He was looking up at the blue sky through the water. The water felt heavy and oppressive, like he had too many clothes on and was being weighed down by the water-saturated garments. No matter what he did, he could not rise up and get to the surface to breathe. He decided to discard his clothes. He felt a freedom when he released them.

He looked down and saw the clothes floating down to the floor of the body of water pulled by their own weight. Free of the anchors of clothing, Billy was able to swim to the air. As he approached the surface, a figure was above him. It looked as if a man was looking down at him, urging him to make it to the surface. The man reached his hand down into the water and helped him when he was close.

At first the dream seemed very real, but Billy quickly realized he was under water for a very long time. The reality of the situation was also confounded by the man reaching to help him. The way he was positioned, he must have been standing on top of the water. How could this man be floating on his feet? There was no boat or rocks near him. He was in the middle of the water by himself, reaching down to help Billy.

Billy reached the surface of the water and gasped for air. As he did so, he was unable to see the man who had helped him, as the sun was behind him and made it impossible to see his face. It was a man for sure, though, and he was standing on the surface of the water. Thinking the situation was a dream, Billy tried to stand on the water. He had seen a television show while he rotted on the couch one night about dreams.

The experts said that if you are unsure of whether or not you are in a dream, you should try to do something extraordinary. If you can do something that would be impossible to do while you were really awake, you are dreaming. The example the experts gave was flying. People who can fly in their dreams know they are dreaming. Billy thought that standing on water was pretty extraordinary. He tried to stand on the water. He imagined it as if it were thick glass to gain his belief and courage. Sure enough, he was standing on it. He looked to the man who had helped him, but he was no longer there. He was turned and walking away from Billy.

Billy thought that since this was a dream for sure and he was able to stand on the water, he could walk on it too. He started walking with ease toward the man. He then started to run so he could intercept him. The water splashed by his feet as he proceeded. The man was only a few yards from him now. Billy caught up to him.

"Hello, thank you for helping me out of the water," said Billy to the man who stopped when he heard Billy's voice.

The man slowly turned. As he did, Billy realized who the man was. It was Jesus. When he turned, his eyes locked with Billy. Dream or not, Billy was overcome with awe. Jesus's eyes peered right at him, and Billy felt like they pierced through him, passed his brain, and touched the back of his skull. He could feel his feet slipping and being pulled downward. He was no longer able to do the extraordinary.

He tried to speak again and say something to Jesus. No words came out, and he took in a mouthful of water as his body sank deeper into the water. Jesus was still looking deeply at him as his eyes finally submerged. The pressure on Billy's lungs became greater. His chest was on fire. He was scrambling to make his way back to the surface, but no matter what he did, he just sank further. Even though a human body normally floats a little in water, and gravity's power is less effective, Billy was sinking faster than what seemed normal even for a dream.

Jesus was still looking down at him, standing on top of the water. The pain of holding his breath was too great to bear. Billy's feet touched the bottom, and he instantly awoke from the dream, gasping for air and coughing violently at the same time.

Balthazar woke up from his deep sleep. Billy's coughing and heavy breathing were like an alarm clock from modern times. Balthazar awoke, gathered his bearings and saw his friend struggling to gain control of his breathing.

"Billy, are you all right?" Balthazar asked as he came to Billy's aid.

"Balthazar, you are not going to believe me, but I think Jesus was reaching out to me in a dream. I was in a body of water, looking up at the surface. I had to shed my clothes because they were too heavy and were weighing me down. I was able to swim to the surface. A man who was standing on the water helped pull me out, and I was able to stand on the water too. He walked away from me, but I chased him down. When the man turned, I realized it was Jesus. I was taken aback as he looked at me. His glance was powerful and sent me back into the water. I sank to the bottom and woke up choking for air. What do you think the dream means?"

"I think it means we are closer to finding Jesus. God's plan is beyond our comprehension. God reveals what he wants to us to help us. It seems to me that we have been struggling. Struggling to find food. Struggling spiritually. God is telling us we are close and should not give up. I think it also means we should go back to the Sea of Galilee. It is the closest body of water to us. Let's go back toward Capernaum."

After Billy felt better and recovered fully from the dream, the two men gathered their things and headed toward Capernaum. The men knew the city and felt comfortable going there minus the fact that a creature had tried very hard to attack them while they were there and again as they headed toward Cana. Jesus had removed that demon from its human victim, but it seemed bent on revenge when they encountered it in the cave. Billy was fearful it would seek them in Capernaum again.

Balthazar, able to see Billy's concern on his face said, "Billy, we cannot worry about the creature we saw in the cave. Jesus has reached out to you in a dream. We need to go to the Sea of Galilee to see if Jesus is calling us there with what was shown to you."

The two men set out on foot toward Capernaum. It was about midday. The sun was directly overhead. Both men were famished. Balthazar reminded Billy that the Sea of Galilee, especially by Capernaum, had fish. It gave both of them purpose as they went to the city. Both the promise of food and the chance to see Jesus gave them a spring in their step. It was these two new variables and perhaps the long night of sleep they had, though it was interrupted by Billy's dream, that urged them forward. They were both down on their luck, and now they were feeling hope again.

It was nighttime when the men arrived. They went to the well where Balthazar and Billy were to originally meet when they separated there earlier. They both filled their skins with water and immediately began to look for food. The vendors who usually occupied that area were not there because it was nighttime. The two men then made their way to the water, where they hoped to find a fisherman who would part with some fish for them. Balthazar had been more frugal with his money. Many people had been extremely generous to the two of them on their trip, but they were so hungry that they were willing to pay for the fish.

At the water's edge, a group of fishermen sat on the shore around a fire. Balthazar and Billy could smell fish cooking on the fire, and their intuition was confirmed as they approached the camp. The men heard them coming, and one of them stood up to confront them.

"Who is that approaching?" the man said as he pulled out a knife.

Balthazar quickly responded, "We mean no harm, friends. We are weary travelers who are in search of food. We would be willing to pay for some of your catch and to share your fire."

Balthazar took his sword from his scabbard, turned it around, and offered it to the group, showing he meant no harm. The men allowed them to join them. There was plenty of fish and bread to go around. It had been a long time since Billy and Balthazar had a solid meal. One of the men showed them how they were cooking the fish.

They had taken medium-size rocks and made a bed underneath the hot coals of the wood that had been burning. They then took the fish and placed them on the coals, covering them up with a second set of stones so the fish would not burn but would roast like in a small oven. The men had used herbs as a rub on the fish, and that aroma drew the two men into the camp. The smell of the herbs flavoring the fish was worth approaching the strangers in the dark.

As the men became acquainted, the fishermen told Billy and Balthazar earlier that day they heard of a man named Jesus who performed a strange miracle. All the fishermen were impressed by the story. They all told parts of the story and added more to it if something was missed. Jesus had been speaking to a large crowd nearby. As the day grew later, his disciples told him that the people would need to find something to eat. Jesus told his men to feed the group instead. Jesus's disciples were confused. It would take a lot of food to feed the group, as it was very large. Jesus told them to gather what food they had.

It became obvious that there was not enough food for all the people. They had some fish and a little bread. The disciples feared the worst. Jesus said a prayer and told them to distribute the food. To their amazement, there was enough food for everyone. Jesus performed a miracle. The men had not seen Jesus yet but were hopeful they would get a chance to, since he remained in the area. They all believed he was the Son of God.

Billy and Balthazar quickly explained during the meal that they had been tracking Jesus and trying to meet him. They let the fishermen know they, too, were believers. The fishermen were impressed with the zealous efforts of Billy and Balthazar. They could not believe that the two men had spent all that time looking for Jesus after all of the challenges they had been through.

Balthazar reached into his coin sack and went to pay the fishermen. All of them thanked him for offering to pay, but they wanted to share their bounty without cost. The fishermen and the travelers talked after supper. A member of their outfit came new to the fire, carrying provisions, rope, and more. He had been in the city to get what they needed. He said that on his way back he saw some of Jesus's disciples getting ready to take a boat on the water.

Jesus was not with them. He spoke to them briefly about the miracle. The disciples who had been with Jesus for a while were as amazed as anyone by the food being multiplied and the people being fed. The new fisherman told all of them that the count of people that were fed with a few fish and loaves of bread was five thousand. This made the miracle even more astonishing.

Billy and Balthazar looked at each other. They quickly gathered their things. The fishermen were disappointed that they were leaving. Billy explained their hastened departure. If they were to catch up with Jesus, they could not linger. The fishermen told them that if they needed help, especially with travel, they would help by giving them a ride in their boats.

"We can't thank you enough for the food and your generosity. Thank you, our new friends," said Billy.

"Where did you say the disciples were last seen?" asked Balthazar.

"Just down the shore over there," said the fisherman who just arrived at the camp.

The men all said goodbye and Billy and Balthazar headed to find the disciples. There was no one on the shore as they walked along, but they noticed a lone boat out on the sea. The men were struggling to row. Since Billy and Balthazar had left the camp of the fishermen, a fierce wind had picked up and a storm had begun to blow in from across the sea, pushing the men who were attempting to row against the wind backward.

Both Billy and Balthazar stopped to see if it was the disciples in the boat. It was very dark. Only the moon shone on the water, allowing a glimpse of the silhouette of the boat on the rough seas that were getting rougher. The light of the moon was also dissipating as clouds were brought in from the strong winds.

Down the shore to the right it looked as if there was a light moving out onto the water. Billy and Balthazar walked toward it. As they got closer, they both assumed it was another boat launching onto the sea. They thought it odd for a boat to be launching with the weather getting so challenging. They were at the spot on the shore where the boat should have been in the water, but there was no boat and the light was not a light.

It was a person.

It was Jesus.

Jesus was giving off a radiance as he walked on the water. Both men looked at each other in amazement. Jesus was walking on water. He was walking out to the boat in the middle of the storm. Just as he did in Billy's dream, Jesus drew closer to the boat. One of the men tried to get out of the boat and come to Jesus. He went directly into the water. Jesus helped him and as both of them climbed into the boat, the wind completely died down and the storm was gone as quickly as it had come.

Billy was reminded immediately of his dream. He was drawn to this moment and was supposed to see Jesus walk on the water. This is what the dream was telling him. The dream was telling him he would be present and witness Jesus miraculously walking on the sea. Jesus and his disciples headed away from shore and out across the water. The fisherman who saw the light and came to investigate walked up behind them.

"Did you see him walk on water?" some of the men asked.

"We did see. Did you see the light he gave off?" said Billy.

"The miracles are truly real. He is really the Son of God," said one of the fishermen in amazement.

Billy convinced the fishermen to take their boat and follow Jesus and his disciples. It took a little bit of time for the men to organize, but they set off after them. In the dark, they were unable to see Jesus's boat. Billy kept his eyes open, looking for the light that Jesus gave off, but could see nothing. They were piloting the boat blind to where the other boat was headed. Balthazar went to the front of the boat and prayed. He prayed for God to give them guidance.

"Our Lord and heavenly Father hear our prayer. We search for your son on earth and seek your guidance. We are lost on the seas and in need of your direction. Grant us your sight. Give us your wisdom," said Balthazar.

The moon began to shine again as clouds left the night sky. The moonlight revealed the shadow of a boat in the far distance. Assuming the boat was that of Jesus and the disciples and the answer to Balthazar's prayer, the fishermen turned the boat in that direction. Jesus's boat was moving a lot faster than the fishermen's boat. Though they could see them, they could not gain ground on them, and the distance between them grew until they could not see the boat at all. Billy and Balthazar felt the pain of losing another chance to meet Jesus.

"There is no need for us to see where the boat is; there is only one place it can be going. The city of Gennesaret is where they are headed. It is directly in front of us," said one of the fishermen.

The sun was beginning to rise as they continued after the other boat. They reached the shore and saw a crowd forming just inland. They knew the people congregated to see Jesus. Word of his actions and miracles had spread across the territory, and believers were flocking to see if the rumors were true.

As they brought their boat to shore, the men noticed some of the people who were moving toward the crowd were carrying other people. And as they drew even closer, they saw they brought the sick and injured before Jesus. The scene was overwhelming. Many of the people seemed desperate and were crying out to Jesus to help their loved ones. Billy reached the mob first. As the group pushed closer to Jesus, Billy strained to see him but couldn't. He went to another side of the crowd for a different look. The crowd moved like waves back and forth, pushing and pulling as the people tried to get closer to Jesus.

Billy finally saw him. He saw Jesus standing in the middle of this chaos. Jesus turned his head sharply in Billy's direction and did not take his eyes off him as Billy struggled through the other people trying to get closer. He could see Jesus, and Jesus could see him. Billy was almost there and less than an arm's length away from Jesus.

Jesus reached his hand out toward Billy. Just as they were about to touch, Billy was pushed back by the crowd as the wave of people shifted. A man to his left lost his footing and surged into Billy. Billy was struck in the head by a hard part of the man's body. The crowd shifted again, and Billy fell. Feet trampled Billy, and he was knocked unconscious.

CHAPTER 12

SPLIT

While he was knocked out, vivid visions played in Billy's mind. Snapshots of his childhood days in Sunday school and real moments captured like a picture. They were images of Jesus. At first they were glimpses of drawings and paintings Sunday school teachers used to illustrate a story they were telling. Paintings of Jesus coming into Jerusalem on Palm Sunday, or the crowd cheering for him and placing the branches of palms and their clothes as he made his way into the city. Sights of Jesus bloodied and hanging on a cross. Roman soldiers rushing out of the city gates. A nervous man speaking with other men in adorned robes. The same man kissing Jesus on the cheek.

As the man kissed Jesus on the cheek, Jesus's eyes were closed. His eyes opened, and there was clarity to the moment as a dream. Billy felt Jesus's eyes deep into his mind as Jesus left a verbal imprint saying his name.

Billy immediately awoke to Balthazar propping his head up with a travel bag. Billy had a sharp pain in his head, and his body was stinging as well from being stepped on by the crowd, but he was alive. Everyone was gone. Billy sat up with his arms over his midsection, which hurt the most.

"Jesus?"

"Gone," said Balthazar.

"Balthazar, I believe Jesus has reached out to me. I just had a vision. I don't know for sure, but the vision was of Jesus in the city of Jerusalem. As you know, I have some knowledge of Jesus's history from my time. Most of the things we are experiencing have been written down into a book. I remember teachers showing us pictures of Jesus's key stories. Those moments were just reshown to me, along with some vivid images of Jesus that were not from my past, but I recognized them as part of Jesus's story. The time is coming where he will go to Jerusalem and finish his ministry. I believe Jesus showed me this because that is where I am to meet him. I am convinced: Jerusalem is where we must go."

"Billy, you and I have become very close. I believe you have a very close connection with God and hopefully with Jesus. I do feel strongly that we should continue after Jesus where we know he is traveling. Yes, he may ultimately arrive in Jerusalem, but with the information we have on hand we may catch him first in Tyre," said Balthazar.

"Balthazar, I disagree with you. There are two ways to look at this situation. I feel like we have been chasing a rabbit that is one or two steps quicker than us, and we know that Jesus is heading to Jerusalem eventually, and we can be the hunter that waits for the rabbit there. The way we have been going about this has allowed us some opportunities, but I think the vision is telling us to head to Jerusalem," said Billy, needing Balthazar to help him to his feet.

"Maybe we can employ both methods. What if I take you to Jerusalem? I will then continue after Jesus. If what you say is true, he will lead me there anyway, if I do not catch up with him first. And if I do intercept him, I will stay with him as a follower and get word to you of our location. My grandfather also had visions. In my experience, the visions were mostly intended for him and his interpretations. Unfortunately, I did not receive the sight that my grandfather was blessed with and maybe you are blessed with. Think about the dream you had of Jesus walking on water." said Balthazar. "I believe you must follow your vision, and my approach must be to track Jesus."

The two men agreed they would travel together to Jerusalem and then part ways in an effort to use both methods of finding Jesus. They were sad to eventually separate, but as anyone knows, distance does not ruin friendships unless the friends no longer wish to stay close. The two had differing opinions on how to accomplish the same goal and wanted to try both methods. They both hoped one of them was right, and there was comfort in multiple solutions to the problem of finding Jesus rather than worry one of the ideas was folly.

Billy especially respected the opinion of Balthazar, which a vision was to be interpreted by the one who received it. Because of this, Billy was convinced he should follow his own path and wait in Jerusalem. He could keep his senses open waiting for the arrival of Jesus. Meanwhile, Balthazar could actively seek Jesus and stay moving. Both opportunities led to Jerusalem.

Before they could set off on the road to Jerusalem, Billy needed some medical attention. As a magi, Balthazar was knowledgeable in healing. Billy was hurt badly. After examining him, Balthazar concluded he was not in any immediate danger. He would be all right with a bit of rest and some curing. Balthazar made Billy comfortable and then told him to get some rest while he procured a few things.

Billy was resting on his back when Balthazar returned. Billy watched him combine figs, pomegranate juice, and olive tree leaves with some other potent herbs he had gathered or had with him in his travel bags. Balthazar made a paste that he spread where Billy was cut and bruised. They were lucky that all was not lost during the incident at the cave. Immediately, Billy felt some relief and comfort from Balthazar's ointment.

"I am grateful to be traveling with a magi. Maybe we shouldn't split up," Billy said, smiling as best he could with the pain.

"My father had a gift for healing. I watched and listened as he would apply his knowledge. This wisdom is ancient and has been passed down for many years. But you are right: you need me," Balthazar said, laughing. "We are also in good fortune, my friend. When I went to gather supplies for the journey and get some healing materials for your contusions and injuries, I met with a man who is headed to Jerusalem to deliver figs to vendors. He must get there quickly so they don't spoil. He has room in his cart for you to lay down. You can heal and rest."

Billy was grateful for his thoughtfulness. It would be at least a day before Billy could travel on foot by himself. The crowd must have trampled him when he went unconscious. He felt better when Balthazar applied his ointment, but he felt pain when the two men latched on to a side of his impermanent bedding and lifted him into the cart.

He was comforted again as they laid him down, and Balthazar applied a second dose of the balm. Billy likened what Balthazar was applying to the equivalent of modern-day IcyHot, but it smelled significantly better. Billy was surrounded by figs. The aroma was pleasant. He drifted off to sleep. Balthazar climbed up on the front of the cart with the driver, and they were off to Jerusalem.

It was over one hundred miles from Gennesaret to Jerusalem. The trip went quickly for Billy, who slept in the cart. Balthazar made a tent to cover himself to protect him from the sun as he rested. They stopped three times a day to feed the animals pulling the cart, treat Billy's wounds, eat some food, and go to the bathroom. They would leave just after sunrise, and they would travel until it started becoming dark. Billy stayed in the cart overnight in his makeshift hospital bed, and the driver and Balthazar would make a camp like Billy and Balthazar had done many times before. Billy never left the cart, except to relieve himself. Balthazar's ointment worked. Billy healed quickly as they moved toward Jerusalem.

In the late afternoon of the fourth day of travel, the group arrived and entered through the sheep gate on the eastern side of the city near the Garden of Gethsemane, just south of the Kindron Valley. They passed from the north, going around the high towers on Josephus's north wall. The north wall had limited entrances strategically. Almost all the entrances for common people were on the eastern side of the city. Just south of the entrance was the temple. The synagogue was much larger than the other cities they had been to.

The travelers parted ways with the fig farmer. They expressed their gratitude to the man for being so generous. Because of his ride in the cart, Billy was able to heal. Billy tested his legs as they waved to the cart driver as he drove away. He was in much better physical condition than he expected.

"Thank you, Balthazar. There is no way I would have recovered this quickly without your help, and I appreciate you getting us a ride," said Billy.

"My friend, you would have done likewise for me. Come with me. We need to get you lodging before I leave you by yourself."

They moved passed the temple and into the city. Balthazar had been on trips to Jerusalem before and knew some people in the market. They stopped and spoke to some of the shop owners. Balthazar had a plan to get Billy both a job and a place to live at the same time, if possible. Several shop owners had positions available but nowhere to live or vice versa. Looking for an ideal situation, they started looking in some places that were less familiar. One of the blacksmith forges was looking for an apprentice, according to one of Balthazar's friends. They approached the workshop Balthazar's friend suggested. A young man greeted them.

"What can I do for you, gentleman?" the bright young man said, "My name is Eran. I am an apprentice to the head blacksmith here."

"We were told your master may be looking for another apprentice. Is this true?" asked Balthazar.

Eran went back to the shop, remembering he needed to finish a small task. He motioned the men to come into the shop. The heat was noticeable and intense. Balthazar and Billy had droplets of sweat form on their foreheads. Eran finished his small job, putting his tools back in order.

"My master is looking for another apprentice, not two."

"I am actually the one looking for the position," said Billy. "My name is Billy, and this is Balthazar."

Just then the master returned. Eran introduced the men to him, and the master was excited to discuss the opportunity with Billy. The man's name was Tehan. The head blacksmith had been in the city for many years. He knew Balthazar's father and grandfather. Balthazar failed to recall Tehan being talked about by anyone in the family, but his father and grandfather knew many people.

He had met them when they had traveled to the city many years ago, when Balthazar was too small to travel. He spoke very highly of them both and said he found them to be honorable men. It was fortuitous that the head blacksmith knew of Balthazar's father and grandfather. Everything seemed to be falling into place.

Tehan seemed a pleasant man. He was shorter than six feet tall and thicker than most men. One could tell he had been swinging a heavy hammer his entire life. His arms looked like they had been chiseled by his own tools.

"Do you know of anyone looking for a boarder as well?" said Balthazar.

"We have the one position for an apprentice. It is hard work. The job is yours, Billy, if you would like it. I must get back to something I have been working on. I needed to get this tool to finish, but now I am on a tight schedule. I believe Eran is the one to talk to about a potential place to stay," said Tehan.

Eran looked at the ground for a moment and said, "I believe I may have a place available for you. My brother passed away last year. He stayed with my wife, Anna, and me, with our two children. We rented the place with the idea of sharing the cost. The last year has been very difficult for us. I will need to speak with my wife, but if she agrees, you will have a place to stay. We are humble and simple people. It is not much, but you will have a place to eat and sleep."

"I am almost finished. Let me help Tehan with this last project he needs to finish, and we can meet with my wife, and you can see the place."

Tehan was busy in the back of the shop. He was finishing an engraving on a weapon. The tool he had gone to get was specifically used for engraving. Many men in the cities could make pots and pans, weapons, and other metal pieces, but the most talented of all the blacksmiths were those who could also adorn and enhance the piece. Looking at Tehan, it was hard to believe he was capable of such artistry, but Balthazar and Billy looked on as he performed the exquisite design.

As they watched Tehan work, Billy thought of his own lack of talent and inability to do a good job at anything. He saw what Tehan was doing with admiration and reserved in his mind that he was going to focus and do his best for Tehan and for Eran and for Balthazar, whose family name had landed him this job.

Billy had changed so much during his time in Jesus's world. He realized his transformation began the minute he landed there. He was forced to take on the challenge of the leopard. Billy never could have done that by himself. He made friends and traveled. He searched for the Son of God. He crossed demons. He had witnessed Jesus walk on water.

Physically, Billy was stronger and more fit. Spiritually, Billy regained faith and grew emotionally. Billy had purpose to all things that were important to him, including his family and getting back to them. Billy had a newfound energy in his heart and soul. He had become a good friend to Balthazar. He now had a job in the world of Jesus and would soon be meeting him.

Tehan finished his delicate work on the weapon. When finished, the three other men admired it as he held it up. It was a short scourge with a metal handle fashioned with leather string for grip. On the top of the metal handle was the name of the soldier, his legion's symbol, and rank. There was a hole at the top of the handle where leather strips holding sharp and shiny metal square pieces on the end of it reminded the men that the weapon was a painful reminder of the power of Rome. Anyone who would have that scourge across their flesh would be scarred for life. The weapon was both beautiful in design and horrible in its purpose.

"I am off to deliver this to a soldier at the jail. He is giving this to a newly promoted comrade. I can't believe I was able to finish it on time. If you are with us, I will see you tomorrow morning, Billy," said Tehan. "Please close up the shop, Eran. Good night."

Billy and Balthazar helped to close down the shop on Eran's commands. The three men were able to do so quickly, and soon they were on their way to Eran's house to meet with Anna, his wife. Their house was not too far away from the blacksmith shop. It was a simple abode in a simple neighborhood. There was nothing special or ornamental about the dwelling.

All the brick and mortar the buildings were made of looked the same. It would be difficult for Billy to recognize the right home on his first solo chance to locate it, if he was given the opportunity. The family had the lower part of the building. Another family lived upstairs. As they approached the door, Eran stopped them and asked that they wait outside while he talked to his wife.

Standing outside and looking at a closed door, the two friends looked at each other and smiled as Eran's wife, Anna, could be heard yelling at Eran. Eran spoke in a soft tone, almost pleading with her. They could not hear a word he was saying, but they heard every word she was saying and so could anyone within one hundred yards. The people upstairs came to their window to see what the ruckus was below, and several other neighbors came to windows and doors to listen, as it was entertaining.

After a few minutes of the same, the door opened, a simple but beautiful woman came out and offered the men to come inside the house. She looked up at her neighbors with a stern face and they scattered back into their homes as quickly as they had originally come out. She was the last to enter the house and closed the door with a lot of energy to let the neighbors know that the fight with her husband was none of their business.

Inside, Anna had made extra places for the two guests. She was a modest woman in appearance and personality, though pretty. Her dark hair and eyes matched each other and gave her a striking appeal. She was above average height—somewhere over five foot seven. Two children popped around the corner from a bedroom. Both had very long hair that was as dark as their mother and father's. One of them had curly hair like their father, and the other had straight hair like their mother. Both of them were young, perhaps six and four.

She apologized for raising her voice at her husband. With modesty, she said that their private moments and especially arguments were hard to keep between them with such thin walls. As strangers, they should not have heard their words.

"I am not sure my wife would be happy with me if I brought two strangers home with me and asked if one of them could live with us," said Billy. "Your reaction and anger is quite understandable. Please forgive us that we were privy to your private conversation. My name is Billy."

"Thank you for your kind words. My name is Anna. The two boys are Kinah," as she presented the curly haired boy, "and Shem."

"We are grateful that you have welcomed us into your home. My name is Balthazar. We must be leaving to look for accommodations. We are sorry for inconveniencing you."

"Nonsense," said Anna. "You are welcome here. Please join us for dinner. We can discuss Billy staying here. Please sit down with us at the table."

The meal was simple but delicious. Anna made a lentil stew spiced with cumin and served with olives, goat cheese, and bread. The bread was incredible. Billy noticed a small oven in the same room near a cooking area. The main room was large and stored a lot of the family's possessions.

"This bread is delicious," said Billy.

"Anna makes the best bread. Her bread fetches a good price in the market. Vendors buy it from her and sell it on the streets," said Eran.

Balthazar explained to Anna that he would be leaving in the morning. He had business elsewhere in the region, but Billy alone would be staying with them and working at the blacksmith's shop. He did his best to vouch for Billy's character. Billy had never heard Balthazar speak as he did. Billy thought Balthazar would make an excellent salesman in his time and world.

As Balthazar conversed with Eran and Anna, Billy watched the children. He watched their small movements. He was reminded of his children. Billy's daydreamed about being at the dinner table with his own children. He imagined asking them about their days and what they had going on in their lives.

He imagined his kids asking him questions and advice, and he shared his knowledge with them. He was helping them. He loved them, and they knew it. He felt sad that he was not with them and wished he had been a better father. If given a second chance to see them and be with them, he would make a difference and love them like no other parent had loved their children.

A tear rolled down Billy's cheek as he fantasized and looked at Anna's and Eran's children. They were loved by their parents and were comfortable in this environment. They were respectful and quiet at the table. Anna and Eran were good parents, and it showed in the way their children behaved.

Billy's kids were wonderful. His wife was the one responsible for their respect and qualities. He had nothing to do with their rearing. He imagined how amazing and talented they would be if they had a second parent reinforcing what she had already done a great job of doing.

Anna noticed Billy's tears and said, "Do you have children of your own, Billy?"

"Yes," Billy said as he wiped the tears from his face.

"My friend has been gone from his family for an extended amount of time, and they are far away from him," said Balthazar.

"And you, Balthazar?" asked Eran.

"Yes, I have children as well. They are God's greatest blessing."

Anna wiped her mouth, cleared her throat, and said, "We would be honored if the two of you would spend the night. Our home is small. We have this room where the two of you can sleep tonight. In the back, the one extra room was turned into two rooms when Eran's brother lived with us, but the children sleep their now. It is not much, but you will have a place to stay."

Balthazar and Billy expressed their thanks. After supper, everyone helped clean up the kitchen and table. Billy noticed how much of a family Eran, Anna, and the boys were, and he longed for his own home. Billy and Balthazar moved the table slightly and set up their mats in the far corner of the house. The children politely said good night to them and hurried off into the small room they shared. Anna and Eran, Eran with his arm around Anna, said good night to them as well and checked on the children before heading to sleep as well.

"You know, this is one of the best situations we have been in for sleeping accommodations since I met you," said Billy.

"We are blessed. I am happy for you, my friend. I can leave tomorrow knowing you have a good situation," said Balthazar.

"I hope one of us is able to find Jesus," Billy said. "I have so many questions."

"I believe our patience will reveal better fortune for us in the near future. Let us sleep and pray for good fortune as I search and as you wait."

Billy turned toward the wall, closed his eyes, and prayed, "Dear God, please bless my family. Keep them safe, happy, and healthy while I am away. Bless Balthazar as he continues our quest to find your son. Thank you for the blessing of my new job here in Jerusalem and newfound friends. Please keep Eran, Anna, and their children in your blessings. Finally, if it be your will, reveal your plan to me. Reveal your son to me that I may know the path you wish me to follow. Amen."

CHAPTER 13

JERUSALEM

Early the next morning, Balthazar woke Billy, and the two men organized their makeshift beds and moved the table back to where it was originally the night before they moved it to make room for themselves to sleep. Eran and Anna were early risers. They tried to get breakfast situated before the children awoke. Eran prepared breakfast while Anna made some of her signature bread.

Balthazar noted it was unusual in this region for the man to help with food preparation. Eran and Anna were a progressive couple for their time. They viewed each other as equals. The entire house smelled like a gilded bakery by the time she had a few loaves in the oven. With the food Eran was making, everyone was ready to eat.

Breakfast included fresh, warm bread, fruits, and cheese. The meal was very good. The two men were not as hungry, but Balthazar knew he had a long journey in front of him, and Billy knew he would need to work hard to impress his new boss at the blacksmith shop.

After breakfast, the men parted ways. Balthazar was not accustomed to lingering when there was work to be done, and Billy was eager to start his new job. The men embraced quickly. Billy reminded him he would be listening for information on Jesus's arrival. Balthazar reminded Billy he would be sending word if he came in contact with Jesus. The men said farewell and Godspeed one more time, then parted ways.

Balthazar headed west toward the temple. He would leave the city through the numerous gates on that side of town where they had come in earlier with the fig dealer. Billy watched him walk down the street, which was beginning to get crowed as people from Jerusalem were beginning to stir, and commotion would soon be prevalent.

Eran kissed Anna, Kinah, and Shem goodbye, and then he and Billy headed into the blacksmith shop. They arrived before Tehan. Eran showed Billy how to open up the shop. They started fires and prepared for the day's work. Tehan was close behind them and arrived shortly thereafter.

Tehan said to Billy, "You passed your first test. You are on time. Eran is always early. Watch how he does things, and you will know how I like things done."

Tehan took his cupped right hand and patted Eran on his right shoulder as he stood behind him. Eran smiled. He enjoyed pleasing Tehan and appreciated the respect he was shown in return for his efforts. Tehan made it clear that if he passed, the shop would belong to Eran. Eran had progressed quickly in his apprenticeship. He was one of the more skilled and accomplished blacksmith apprentices in the city, but his best quality and attribute was his relationships with people.

People in the city and customers of the blacksmith shop liked Eran. Eran made a point to talk to people, remember names, and prior conversations. He had a knack for customer service and over time, Billy saw how it brought business to them. Tehan was right, Billy was someone he could learn a lot from not just as a blacksmith, but as a person. Billy was fortunate to have come across such a unique and valuable person.

One day when Eran was gone from the shop on an errand for Tehan, he took him aside to tell Billy something important. Tehan made sure that no one else was in the shop. He also looked into the street to make sure no one was close enough to hear what he was about to tell him.

"About a year ago, Eran and his brother Remmen were both working for me. They all lived together in the house where you are staying. Remmen, like Eran, was well liked and had a very personable disposition. Our customers liked him, and Eran's kids worshiped him. He was taller and more physical than Eran. He looked like he should be a soldier. His face was chiseled, as if from stone, and he had a chin that looked unbreakable. Eran looked up to him like a father.

"Their parents had passed away and the two were all the other had before Eran was married and had children. Remmen never married, though many families tried to arrange opportunities for him to marry their daughters. He was waiting. We did not know for what he was waiting, but he was waiting. He was focused on his work and was first in line to take my place here if I should retire or pass away. Eran was proud of his brother and loved him dearly. The situation was ideal for all of them. Eran and Anna benefited from him living with them," said Tehan.

He quickly looked around again to make sure there was still no one listening. "Remmen was an honorable man. He stayed away from trouble and was a community leader. One day a group of men congregated outside the temple to discuss some trouble citizens of Jerusalem were having with the Roman soldiers. It was a peaceful discussion. Leaders were looking for ways of communication with the Roman faction to improve relations and lower anger and hostility for recent arrests and events. Remmen and Eran were headed to the temple to pray and make a small sacrifice. The crowd had grown. There were now many men congregated as Eran and Remmen walked by. The discussion started to become heated, as there were men from both sides of the issue. Some of the men were sympathetic to the Jewish side. Other men were more on the Roman side. One man became very frustrated. It was said that a strange-looking man who was pale and was not recognized by others was talking to him before he became enraged, almost pushing him to his frenzy.

"The man separated himself from the group and drew a knife. Seeing this, Remmen went to subdue him, though he had nothing to do with the discussion or the argument that arose from it. The man felt Remmen step up behind him and turned quickly to confront him. As he did, his knife thrust into Remmen, and he immediately fell. The strange pale man was seen laughing. His dark evil eyes watched Remmen's life force fade away. Many of the people were enraged by his disrespect, both Roman sympathizers and those on the side of the Jewish argument. Some of them threatened the pale man and chased him away from the scene. They did not catch him. Some of the other men, one a physician, attended to Remmen. The knife entered just below the heart. Remmen had lost a lot of blood."

Tehan continued. "As Remmen lay dying, he said to Eran, 'I knew this would happen. For most of my life, I have possessed the gift of foresight. Much of what was revealed to me by God was unimportant. Some of it was useful.' He coughed, blood coming from his mouth. 'I saw my own death but did not know when it was coming and did not know how it happened. I only saw my body lying on the ground, bleeding, and you and the physician kneeling over me. A lot of good knowing this has done me! That is why I did not marry. I did not want to start a family and make a widow.' At the time Eran tried to get Remmen to stop talking to save his breath and energy, but Remmen had more to tell Eran.

'You have been a loyal brother and wonderful husband and father. There is someone coming who you need to help. He will be looking for the messiah, the Son of God. Do everything you can to help him. Use all your resources to help him accomplish his task. God has shown me this. I am not long in this world, Eran.' And as he said that, his eyes became still, and he ceased to breathe. Eran was distraught and laid his body over his brother, holding him. It took Eran a long time to accept what had happened. He was angry with God and everyone and anyone who showed him compassion or sympathy. He grew to hate it because he was so angry about his brother's death. They never caught the man who stabbed him accidentally. Eran eventually came back to work but was not the same. His marriage to Anna suffered. She was not happy, and the entire community was unsure how to approach Eran and Anna. Eran had a temper for anyone who would talk to him. Anna would not make eye contact with anyone.

"I thought you should know this because, Billy, Eran believes you are the one his brother foretold would come to find Jesus. If this is true, you need to know he is thinking about this already. It has taken him a year to get over Remmen's death. He is finally happy again. I saw his energy pick up even more the day you and Balthazar came to the shop."

"I am the man Remmen saw coming. I have been looking for the Son of God for a long time. Because I know Jesus will be coming to Jerusalem, I chose to come to the city to wait for him. I needed a job and a place to stay while I wait and listen for information about him coming to Jerusalem. I believe God led me to you and Eran through Balthazar," Billy said.

The two men continued to talk, though there was much work to do. Because Tehan thought of Eran like a son, he made sure Billy understood how fragile the young man was. He suggested he take Eran for a walk when he returned. During the walk, Tehan recommended Billy tell Eran about his purpose in the city and allow Eran to open up about what Remmen said if he chose to do so. Billy thanked Tehan for his advice and counsel. As soon as they finished their conversation, Eran came down the street at a quick pace to the shop. Eran took his leather apron that was hanging on a hook on the wall, put the top around his neck, and tied the strings behind his back. He saw Billy looking at him strangely.

"What is it, Billy?"

"We need to talk," said Billy. "Tehan, I need to speak with Eran, with your permission."

Looking up from his forge, Tehan swung his hammer with his

right hand and waved an approval with his left. Billy turned to Eran, putting his right hand on his back near his shoulders and ushered him into the street, where they could walk and talk.

"I am here in Jerusalem looking for Jesus. I may have mentioned this to you before; I am not sure," said Billy. "I spoke with Tehan. He said that when your brother passed he told you that he had visions, and one of the visions was of me coming to the city to find the Son of God. I want to tell you that I am that man he saw, and there is more to it. I did not tell you this when I first met you or when we met your family. Do not worry. If I thought I would be a threat to you or your family, I would not have asked to live with you. What I am about to tell you may be shocking. Prepare yourself."

Eran seemed a lot calmer than Billy expected. Eran was expressionless. He looked at Billy, waiting for his revelation.

"I am from the future—far in the future. I have been brought back to your time with the purpose of finding Jesus. I do not know why God wants to me to find him, or what God has planned for me. I met John the Baptist at the Jordan River, and he told me to search for him, as Jesus has a message to tell me. I have been here for a while now. Balthazar and I followed Jesus and missed him several times. We have been so close to meeting and speaking with him. Evil creatures similar to the one that was at your brother's death have chased us. I apologize that I bring it up. I know you were deeply wounded by his passing, but the thing that provoked that man who had the knife was not of this world. His body was, but his spirit was a fallen angel determined to cause havoc and pain in this world for his master. Now that you know the whole story and why I am here, I hope you will still let me stay with you and your family. I will work hard in the shop, help at the house, and you will not even know I am searching for signs and clues of Jesus's whereabouts, as I will not let my personal mission spill out on to you, Anna, or the kids."

Eran stopped walking. He was looking straight ahead as if he was trying to gather himself. He put his hands on his hips simultaneously and turned to Billy.

“The hell with what you said,” said Eran.

“I am sorry if I offended you—” Billy barely got these words out of his mouth before Eran interrupted him.

“You know what happened to my brother.” Eran paced back and forth on the street. “You offend me by not asking me for help. I wish to honor my brother and his final words. I am to help you. I am to use all my powers to make sure your task is fulfilled. Never exclude me again.”

“You must realize there may be some challenges and peril involved in this as we proceed. We are in a Roman-occupied city. Being from the future, I know certain things about what happens to Jesus. Much of what we will encounter will not be pleasant,” said Billy.

“Damn your ignorance.” Eran stepped back. “I meant stop worrying about me. My brother predicted your coming, not my peril from your coming. He would have said something had he foreseen it. We are now brothers. I have felt a kinship from your initial arrival. Tehan probably told you that I struggled for a long time after my brother was gone. Life did not seem important. I do not have the vision like my brother, but I had a revelation in those weeks of mourning. First of all, I have a wonderful wife and family. Secondly, I have a great job with future possibilities. Finally, I have a higher purpose. I did not know you were from the future, as my brother did not tell me this, but I did know you were coming. These three things made me realize I needed to stop feeling sorry for myself and embrace my family and the job I have been blessed with and wait for your arrival. While I have been waiting for you, I have been preparing by developing relationships and listening to conversations and gossip. In other words, I have been ready for you to show up in Jerusalem.”

Billy smiled at Eran and put his hands on his shoulders and then embraced him. Eran embraced him back. The two now had a singular purpose, which was dedicated to finding Jesus. Billy also had another friendship with a being of this time.

Together they would listen and learn of Jesus and his miracles and wait for his arrival in the city. Eran knew many people and made a point of getting among them to hear the rumors. Balthazar was off in the region doing the same reconnaissance on the move. A singular mobile force in Balthazar was out tracking down Jesus, and a two-man crew resided in Jerusalem, living and working but always searching for Jesus. One of the two factions would find Jesus, and hopefully much would be revealed to them.

Months had passed. Billy and Eran heard nothing from Balthazar, and though they heard a lot of rumors regarding Jesus, they never heard of him coming to the city in advance. A few times they would find out that Jesus had visited Jerusalem briefly, and the two men would be incredibly frustrated. But Billy would confide information he knew from the future with Eran, and they would be comforted that Jesus would have a profound arrival that would set off several events that Billy would recognize as their time to find the Son of God.

Billy prayed for his family and for their health and safety. It pained him that he did not know what was happening with them. He would pray for the safety, health, and prosperity of Balthazar, Eran, Anna, Kinah, and Shem. He would pray for forgiveness of the man he used to be—great length and time was spent on this part of his prayers. The words he chose for this part of his prayers were never the same but always centered on regret for what he was and gratitude for the opportunity to change. Billy finished all his prayers, asking for wisdom and knowledge to help him and Eran find Jesus so that he would learn if he could return home or if God had another purpose for him.

As the weeks passed, Billy became an active member in the community. He was well known and respected. He went to temple frequently and prayed. He helped Anna and Eran with the children, and over time had become a brother to Eran. Billy was now blessed to have two close friends in this time.

The two men worked and lived waiting for Jesus. The days ran together and were never dull, as the two of them made the most of their time as they waited. One day a single correspondence arrived at the blacksmith shop in the hands of a traveler from northwestern Samaria one day from Balthazar. Balthazar conveyed that he was close to meeting up with Jesus but had failed to make true contact.

He said in his letter that he prayed Billy would not lose hope, and he felt Billy's decision to go to Jerusalem was a good one. Perhaps they would eventually meet in the city and find Jesus together. Balthazar's words were meant to inspire and bring positivity to Billy, but Billy was already positive and was supported by Eran, Tehan, Anna, and the children.

Billy's faith had grown, and he remained positive God would reveal his plan to him. Although he was a man who was not patient enough to wait through a commercial on television, he would wait Jesus out and do his best to live a positive and healthy life with his newfound friends and family until he arrived.

CHAPTER 14

ARRIVAL

Eran ran into the house and stopped by the table, leaning over to catch his breath, and lifted his right hand to his side, obviously winded and in some discomfort. He raised his left hand as if he wanted to say something but couldn't because of his inability to breathe properly. Eran's wife and children rose to help him, afraid he was ill. Billy got up from the table and his morning breakfast to help his friend. He asked the children to step back and give him some room. He helped Eran into an upright position and had him take his hands and put them over his head.

Billy remembered his father telling him to do so once when he ran his first race for a grade school track meet. Billy never ran the eight-hundred-meter race and found himself in third place on the last turn. Seeing the finish line, Billy kicked into a higher gear and blew past the runners who were in first and second. Billy paid the price for his secondary effort, however, after he crossed the finish line, breaking the ribbon and falling forward. His lungs felt like they were doused with lighter fluid and set ablaze with a match.

His dad was there to watch him compete and saw that he was in distress. Normally, his father would not come out of the stands and onto the track unless he was coaching, but he could see Billy needed help. He immediately picked Billy off the ground and had him put his hands above his head to open his lungs and then had him walk a bit.

Billy had Eran do the same. Raising his hands above his head comforted him, and now Billy had him walking around the table. Eran was able to catch his breath. Soon Eran was ready to speak.

"Jesus entered the city yesterday," Eran said, still trying to catch his breath.

"Jesus is here? All this time waiting, and Jesus is here," said Billy.

Anna was still trying to organize the children after Eran's excited entrance, when she had a thought and said, "Billy, does that mean will you be leaving us?"

"I was told Jesus came into the city, and there was a large crowd. The people were cheering for him, and some even laid down clothing so he would pass without touching the ground. Those who saw him declared he was the Son of God," said Eran.

"Did you hear where he is staying or what he plans on doing?" asked Billy.

"Those I spoke with said he went to the temple after entering the city. That is all I know. I am sorry, Billy."

"Eran, you and Anna have been generous hosts and good friends to me. Never apologize for something that does not need forgiving. I am in debt to you and your family for your generosity," Billy said as he put his hands on Eran's shoulders.

Anna smiled, looking up at the two of them in a moment of friendship. It was good that Billy was with them. Eran lost his older brother the year before and was not himself until Billy arrived. Though Eran and Anna took Billy in, having Billy in Eran's life was equally beneficial. Eran found a friendship with Billy that had been lost with his brother's passing and developed stronger roots as the men worked together, shared meals, and looked out for each other. It was clear that Eran aimed to please Billy and receive his approval, so he found new purpose in helping Billy with getting information on Jesus and his whereabouts.

Anna once described Eran's melancholy after his brother's passing. She described it with sadness as Eran was an energetic and happy man before the accident. Eran questioned his faith and God, never admitting he was angry regarding the accident, but clearly harboring negative feelings after the event. Billy reminded him of his brother and each day their friendship grew. Therefore, Anna was worried that Billy would leave at the announcement of Jesus' arrival into Jerusalem.

Billy saw Eran as a close friend and enjoyed the time they spent together. Billy did not have a sister or a brother, and he enjoyed both the benefit and responsibility of having a little brother in his life. Billy also saw that Eran had fallen into a depression from his brother's death. The looks he had on his face and his body language was familiar to Billy. It was like looking in a mirror after the passing of his father. Billy recognized the body language as the mind, in its infinite ways, struggled to understand and cope with such a difficult moment in one's life while still having the physical presence in this world. Eran was going through a lot when Billy arrived. His arrival was timely and valuable.

"I forgot to tell you something else. I can't believe I forgot to tell you something so important!" Eran said.

"What is it?"

"The men I was speaking with said Jesus had just come from Bethany, east of the city. It is said he performed another miracle. A man passed away—a man named Lazarus. He was the brother of sisters Jesus and the disciples were close to. They told me Lazarus had been gone for some time, apparently for several days. He had been wrapped in burial garments, placed in a tomb, and a stone was placed over the entrance. Jesus, hearing Lazarus was ill, or worse, had already planned to visit but found he was dead. Jesus went to the tomb, asked them to remove the stone, and told Lazarus to come out. Alive and well, Lazarus came from the tomb. Word of this recent miracle filled the city, with men and women telling the story just as I have now. I can't believe I forgot to tell you all of this. This story reached Jerusalem before Jesus; therefore the people cheered him as he entered the city. The Son of God is now seen as the true messiah."

"Can you imagine the joy the family of the dead man felt? He was gone from this earth and entombed. Jesus has them move the stone in front of his tomb and brings him back to life. The man who was dead is now alive and among us. Jesus did this," said Billy.

Eran's wife, Anna, said, "Now that he is in the city, you should be able to find him, Billy. It has been wonderful having you stay with us, but we know your mission has been to speak with him, and your whole purpose of coming to Jerusalem was to wait for his arrival."

"Anna, I have enjoyed spending time with all of you. Being here in this house has reminded so much of my own family. I want to get back to them, if I can. I am hopeful Jesus will allow me an audience and may have a way for me to get back. You know I do not belong here. Well, I didn't belong in my time either. Here I am a stranger because I am not of this age and place. Back where I am from, I made myself a stranger by ignoring the needs of my family and friends and by sinking into my own grief and pain. As much as I love you all, I must get back to my time. I have so much to make amends for."

Eran said, "Billy, you have been a great friend while here and have been as much a part of our family as anyone else who was born into it. I pray you get a chance to go back and show them the man we know you are. They love you already, even though you have not been perfect. That is what families do. They don't look for faults; they look around them. When you get back, you will show them how much you love them. I know you will, and I know Jesus will somehow get you back to them."

"Thank you, Eran. And thank you for all your help and understanding. You could have thrown me out when I told you about what has happened to me, but you didn't. You could have been suspicious, superstitious, or worse, turned me in to authorities."

"God has a plan for all of us. Think of the power he has released on this earth. Is it so different to believe he could make the sun stand still so his armies could continue fighting longer for the sea to part at Moses's and Aaron's command, or for animals to gather in twos on the ark with Noah? No, we believe you. Your story is not hard to fathom if you take into consideration what God has already done on this earth."

After receiving the affirmation of his friends, who had become his newfound family, Billy tried to imagine his time in Sunday school. He tried to remember the story of the crucifixion of Jesus. He remembered that Jesus came into the city and the church called that celebrated day Palm Sunday. He remembered that Jesus and the disciples had the last supper.

He thought about Gethsemane. He would position himself near Gethsemane so that he could try and catch Jesus before his arrest. He strained to remember more but realized that if he were able to discover when Jesus would be in Gethsemane, he could speak with him. This was his best chance. Billy then recalled Judas and his betrayal of Jesus. Judas's disloyalty marked the beginning of the end for Jesus. If Billy could find Judas, he could follow him and get the information about when and where Jesus would be.

Billy and Eran made their way down the east side streets of Jerusalem on their way to work. Both were excited with the thought of Jesus being in town. Billy was energized with the opportunity to meet Jesus, and Eran was eager to help his friend Billy. Work did not seem difficult when their hearts were so light. Working as apprentices in a blacksmith shop where the heat of the region and the heat of the fires and furnace made breathing unbearable, seemed like nothing with something to look forward to. Both Eran and Billy put in a full day's work before their midday break. The head blacksmith noticed their hard work and told them they could leave early that day. As they ate their meager meals at lunch, both men could not help but speculate what might happen in the next few days. It was easy to be encouraged with the news of the arrival of the Son of God.

The men finished up their work that afternoon and were relieved to finish early. As they traveled the short distance back to Eran's home, Billy found a familiar and unwanted feeling creeping into his mind and heart. There was a creature near him. He felt the hair on the back of his neck stand up, and his eyes began to water. He had not seen Balthazar in so long, and he really needed him.

"Eran, please do not ask any questions. Please take what I am carrying and go home. I will be right behind you," Billy said.

Noticing the change in Billy's body language and the departure of bliss from his tone, Eran did not question his friend and started home as Billy asked. He stopped as he turned down their street and looked back from around the corner of a building. He saw Billy squared off with a strange-looking creature.

The creature looked as if it were covered in dust or powder, as it was a pale white color. Its eyes were dark and had dark rings below them. It was dressed according to what it should have on and resembled a human like the others, but it was clear this was something unlike the other human beings who were walking to and fro on the streets. Eran feared for Billy but did not want to upset him by interfering after he asked him to head home. This was a creature similar to the one who spurred the man to kill Remmen.

Billy stood his ground, square to the creature. The creature had strange and peculiar movements, as if there were two beings fighting against each other, and tried to move in Billy's direction. It drew closer to Billy. It was trying to see if Billy would flinch.

"We know you," it said.

"And I know you," said Billy.

"You are the one who seeks the Son of God. My brothers and sisters have followed you and watched you as you have moved among these people like a fish out of water. You know he is here in the city. As we speak, he is engaged with spiritual leaders. They don't like that he has become a religious authority. They had that business sewn up. He is bad for business. he brings hope and truth to the people. The spiritual leaders like the people fearful, like sheep. Like you, Billy, when you encounter my kind. Like you, when you found out your friend lied to you about the talisman. Yes, we have been watching you."

"I am no longer the person who shakes at your kind. My faith is stronger than it was when I first encountered your evil kin. You can only prey on the weak, and I am anything but weak. I have purpose here among these people. I am here for a reason, just like the Son of God. He will wash away your filth. And now that I think of it, you should be afraid, considering he is here in the city. He will remove you like a sliver from this poor soul's body in an instant."

"Well, haven't you grown into a real man? You even wear a man's clothes now and everything. You are still far from home and those you love. My master has sent me to deliver an offer. He will send you back home. All you have to do is commit to him and forget about God and the Son," said the demon.

Billy paused for a moment, contemplating the offer, as it was tempting and said, "Tell your master there are no weak sheep here. There is no depressed and brokenhearted weakling tormented by the death of his father. There is a man of faith in this land. One who does not know all of God's plan, but his faith doesn't waiver because of a false offer from a liar. Now leave me alone and do not return."

"There will not be another offer like this one. Either you take it, or you remain here, far from your family. You will wander looking for the Son of God and never find Him. They have forsaken you. Sometime today one of his disciples will betray him. We have gotten to him. The wheels of our plan are already turning. His disciple's actions will lead to his arrest and death. There is nothing you can do to stop it."

Billy now was starting to remember his Sunday school class lessons a little better now. Judas was to betray Jesus. He needed to find Judas and follow him. He would eventually lead him to Jesus. Billy thought he would stop Judas if he could. Maybe that is why he was sent here. He was to stop Judas. Billy was torn knowing that Jesus's path was to die on the cross; who was he to interfere with the plan of God. It just pained him tremendously to think of the betrayal. It pained him to think of Jesus on the cross.

The demon spoke again, "His disciple will betray him, and the rest will be set in motion. One of ours has been following Judas as well. You should be like him and join us. He is a troubled man. He is not like you. He is greedy."

Eran watched from a distance as his friend spoke with the strange looking creature. Eran thought it strange that no one else noticed the two of them or asked them to move. They were directly in the middle of the street. It looked to Eran as if they were fighting or arguing and Eran was ready in case the encounter became physical. It was difficult for Eran to not help his friend, but he honored his wishes. He felt bad that he did not go home as Billy asked, but he thought he would help in case things escalated.

Billy now a stronger man than in the other encounters, spoke to the demon in a direct tone, "Your plan will not succeed. God will make right the world with his Son as a tool. His Son is a hammer that will crush you and all your kind. For the last time, tell your master the answer is no. My loyalty can't be changed or bought, even if it means I can't get back to my family."

With those words, the demon smirked and slowly withdrew, muttering something Billy could not understand as he stepped away. Billy watched its departure and took a few steps down the street to make sure the demon did not turn and start to follow him. Billy was concerned for Eran and his family. He did not want the demon hurting or scaring them, especially the children. Once the creature was out of sight, Billy turned to head home and saw Eran hiding and watching on the corner of the building. Eran tried to hide quickly, but then stepped out into plain sight as he knew his cover was made obvious.

"I am sorry, Billy. I saw that ghastly creature step up to you, and I stayed to help in case there was an altercation."

"Eran, you are a good friend. And I appreciate the gesture. I did not want you to see that."

"What was that thing? I have seen its kind before. I saw one of them right before my brother was killed.

"That was a servant of Satan inhabiting the poor soul of one of our fellow human beings, too weak to stop it from happening. I pity the person but despise the creature within it. They use the bodies of others to create fear and doubt while spreading the falsehoods of their master. It is my hope that this one will be drawn out by Jesus while in the city. Drawn out with a hammer!"

The two men headed home. Eran was visibly shaken by the encounter with the creature. He talked a little less as they walked, and his face displayed a lowered brow like that when one is deep in thought. Billy saw this and did his best to explain and comfort him as he had several questions and was clearly fearful. Billy told him about his experiences and how he, too, was once afraid of the creatures. He told Eran how the fear they harbor is not healthy, as it adds to the demon's power.

"I learned something from the creature."

"What did he tell you, Billy?"

"The creature said Jesus is with some leaders of the church today. They do not like his presence here in Jerusalem. They are plotting something and one of Jesus' disciples is involved in the plot. I will need to go to the synagogue to see if Jesus or Judas, his disciple, are there."

"I will go with you!" Eran said.

"My friend, this time I am going to ask you to truly honor my wishes. I will walk home with you, and we will part ways for a while. I cannot risk putting your life or the lives of your family in danger. That creature was real, and they have manipulated the events that are in motion. I do not know what other part they play in this, but I know the lives of your family are the most important thing for you to worry about right now," said Billy as they finished the walk home.

CHAPTER 15

JUDAS AND A CREATURE

Billy and Eran entered the simple dwelling, and the kids attacked them with love. Anna, sensing the tension of the men, perhaps after the unnerving experience with the creature in the street, was more apprehensive to come to the men and greet them. Billy asked that he speak with Eran and Anna alone as not to frighten the children.

"I must go to the synagogue in search of Jesus and one of his disciples. I do not know if I will return. I know some things about what is about to unfold because in my time it is history, even though we are presently experiencing it now," said Billy.

Anna began to say, "Why don't you wait—"

Eran interrupted her, "We saw something today in the street that you need to know about before you try and convince Billy to change his mind. An agent of Satan approached Billy today as we walked home in the guise of a poor human being who was being tormented and controlled by the creature. It was a person but obviously affected by the dark being. I saw it happen. Billy stood up to him and sent him away, but he may be back. As much as it pains me, we will need to distance ourselves from Billy as he finishes his quest."

"Abandon him? He needs our help," said Anna.

"You are true friends, and I know you would never leave my side when things were difficult, but for the sake of your children we need to part as I search for them. I will most likely be back, but where I am going may bring danger to your family. I can't have that on my conscience."

Billy hugged Anna and Eran and then the children and walked out the door after looking back at them one more time. Anna was crying and tried not to show it, so Billy would be strong, and Eran gave an approving nod. Billy was glad they did not fuss over his departure. He may find nothing and be back, and then again he may engage with Jesus and find out why he was sent there.

Billy walked down the street toward the synagogue. The synagogue or temple, as many of the citizens of the region called it, was close to Eran's and Anna's domicile. For a moment, Billy had concern regarding the creature he encountered and looked around him. He then drew courage inwardly, as he was able to face it down and make it leave him. He was stronger in his faith than when he first encountered its kind.

The streets of Jerusalem were filled with the sights and smells that he grew accustomed to. Almost everyone in the city made their own food. As one passed by homes, the smell of meat or bread baking filled the streets and made Billy a little hungry. A few vendors sold food in the city. Bread and other baked goods were popular at the stands of the vendors. Billy had some money from working in the blacksmith's workshop, but not much. He bought some bread and a salted meat that might cure his hunger, as he was to be on the hunt for Jesus and Judas.

Billy arrived at the temple. There were a lot of people outside the temple. From what he gathered, Jesus had just been there. He smiled thinking how many times he was going to just miss Jesus, but he accepted the small irony and listened to the conversations of the people about. One of the men looked familiar. He was arguing with another man. He got a little closer but tried to be discrete. The man saw him and recognized him as well. Billy withdrew and put his hood up over his head to conceal himself.

"Friend! Friend, do you remember me? Maybe if I sit down on the ground and get a cup you will give me a coin," the man said, smiling wide.

It was the paralytic man from Capernaum. Billy did not recognize him, because he was standing. Billy was pleased to see him walking and standing.

Trying not to draw attention to them, Billy led the man around a building for cover and said, "Hello, friend, it looks as if your luck has changed for the better."

"There is no luck here. The Son of God has healed me. I am one of those stories you hear of his miraculous works and deeds. I serve him now as many do. He has a group of men and women who follow him. The number is vast and grows daily."

"What has happened here at the synagogue? I saw you were arguing with someone."

"Jesus came to the temple yesterday and rebuked many of the leaders saying they were unworthy to represent God. The temple has become a place where they are more interested in making money than helping people spiritually. Many people are afraid to say anything. They are afraid that they might be persecuted for talking against the powerful leaders. Jesus came here again today. The leaders looked to ensnare him in his words and get him to commit blasphemy so that they could have him arrested. Jesus is not good for the leaders. His truth weakens their position. I fear for Jesus."

"Who was the man you were arguing with? Is he a leader?"

"No, he is not a leader, he is one of Jesus' close disciples. His name is Judas."

Billy said to the man trying not to give away that he was in search of Judas, "I must go, my friend. I am so happy for you that you have been touched by Jesus and are free from your affliction."

"How about you? Have you seen Jesus?"

"I am still searching and that is why I must go. Forgive me for not being able to talk more, but I am in a hurry. Hopefully, I will see you again."

Billy hugged the man. He really was happy for his transformation. For him to be able to walk again had changed his life and now he serves and follows Jesus. Each miracle and event Jesus performed brought notoriety to his name as he traveled. Billy witnessed some of this as he followed in his footsteps, but the stories had taken on a life of their own. This was proven by Jesus' triumphant entrance to the city based on what Eran said.

Billy saw Judas. He stopped in his tracks, afraid to be seen and afraid to move toward him. This was the man of legendary biblical status. The man who was once the close friend and disciple of Jesus and was now contemplating betraying him. Billy moved toward the temple as Judas scurried through the front entrance. Judas looked back and around, as if to see if he was under anyone's watchful eye.

Billy pursued him cautiously. The temple was a place where all sorts of people came to worship. The rich and the poor alike. Outside the temple were numerous vendors selling animals like doves for sacrifice. There were other vendors outside as well. Jesus was right, if the leaders were making money off these sales. There was a lot of consumerism involved with the temple from what Billy could gather.

Judas was walking through the temple toward the back. He looked as if he knew where he was headed. He did not pause to pray or worship. He had another strategy on his mind. There were several heavy curtains in the temple, hanging from the ceiling to the floor. Judas slipped behind one of them to the left, looking first to see that no one would notice. Billy folded his hands and lowered his hands as Judas looked back. Judas continued through the curtains and out of sight.

Billy quickly moved to follow, but took a moment at the curtain to listen in case Judas was talking with someone right behind it. Billy slowly pulled back the curtain a little bit and saw Judas going out a door into sunlight. Judas shut the door behind him as he went outside. Billy quietly and softly stepped toward the door and opened it a crack. Beyond the door was an open courtyard which led to a small sanctuary. Several men dressed in ceremonial robes came from the sanctuary, approaching Judas. As they met, they did not shake hands, but with their hands folded, gave an acknowledging nod for a greeting.

Billy could barely make out what they were saying initially. There was a breeze rustling through the trees that were on the edge and all around the courtyard. As the breeze picked up, Billy could not hear what the men were saying. When the breeze died down, Billy could hear them clearly and distinctly. The timing of the breeze was perfect. Jesus came into town on Sunday and it was now Tuesday. The men offered a bag to Judas. Billy could only assume it was the infamous pieces of silver that Judas was offered to betray Jesus.

"On Thursday, Jesus and all the disciples will be eating a meal for Passover. Afterward Jesus has said that he wants to go to Gethsemane to pray. Deploy the soldiers to Gethsemane and have them wait for our arrival in the garden. Wait for me to give a signal and then move in. I will kiss Jesus on the cheek. This will be the signal," said Judas as he twitched a little, showing he may be under the influence of one of the demons, as the creature stated earlier. This movement Billy recognized all too well.

The men continued to talk. Billy stayed and listened. There was nothing else said that related to Jesus or where he would be or when, but it was important that Billy hear everything in case a new piece of information came up. Billy had some selfish thoughts that were quickly changed as he thought about the implications of what was happening in front of him. At first, Billy could only think about himself and the chance to meet with Jesus.

He did not think about what the kiss meant for the larger picture. Judas' betrayal meant Jesus would be arrested, convicted unjustly, and hung on the cross, where he would die. Billy then felt guilty for his selfish thoughts. Yes, he would like to get back home and to his family, but not when Jesus was set for death. Billy had never met the man, but after trailing after him for so long he felt a kinship to him and the works he had done. He was torn about stopping Judas.

The meeting was over. The men once again bowed to each other, and Judas left the courtyard thirty coins heavier than before. Billy went behind the door as Judas came through. He hid behind the door as it opened. Judas walked through and then went out into the temple through the heavy curtain. After making sure it was clear, Billy followed behind Judas as he walked through the temple and out the front.

Judas hid the coins beneath his robes and hung them on his sash as he walked out into the street. Billy was right behind him. Billy quickened his pace, trying to keep up with him and to eventually overtake him. Billy was still split on whether to stop Judas from committing the betrayal, but his first task was to close the distance.

As he was about five yards behind him, he started to reach out to tap him on the shoulder and confront him, but he was struck by an acute pain as he was attacked and pushed behind a building. Judas looked behind himself as he heard the ruckus only to find an empty street as the sun started to lower itself behind the buildings and the wall of the city.

The streets were darkening as Judas continued his way and Billy looked up to find the creature who had recently confronted him in the street standing over him like a defensive back who had just flattened a wide receiver in punishment for catching a ball in his zone. Billy's head had hit the side of the building as the creature tackled him. He saw the evil thing smiling and looking down at him.

"I told you things are in motion. There is nothing you or anyone can do about it. We will make sure of that. You should have taken the offer from my master. Now, you will never see your family again. Billy, you are bleeding," said the demon as he raised his knee and kicked out with the bottom of his heel into Billy's forehead.

The lights went out for Billy and not just the light of the sun. It was the light that came into his eyes. Unable to see, he felt his body being dragged down the street. It was extremely painful. The streets of Jerusalem were hard and bumpy. Billy tried to wipe his eyes and realized why he couldn't see. Blood was streaming down his face either from where he hit the side of the building or from the creature kicking its heel.

Either way, he could not see and could not clear his eyes of blood. He needed some water and a rag. He tried to put his hands out right and left of his body to anchor himself like a ship, but the creature was surprisingly strong and was unfazed by Billy's efforts. Growing frustrated with Billy's efforts to prevent him, the creature turned and gave a final and definitive kick to Billy once more and he was out.

Billy awoke at sunrise on Wednesday to a familiar voice. It was Balthazar. He was kneeling over Billy with some cloth and a bowl of water. Eran was standing above Balthazar hovering while moving back and forth with a concerned look on his face.

"Who did this to you?" Eran asked as Balthazar turned to calm him.

"Please, be still, young man. He will be all right," said Balthazar.

"One of Jesus's disciples named Judas was in the temple. We had heard that he planned to betray Jesus from one of the demons that torment me, as you know, from time to time. He met us on our way home from work and tried to get me to join them in trade for a chance to go back home to my family. I said no. While he offered me the chance to go back, he let it slip that one of Jesus's disciples was with them, influenced by the devil's powers, and that things were set in motion, leading to Jesus's demise," Billy said as he tried to sit up.

"I followed Jesus to Jerusalem. As always, I was always right behind him. I have been lucky to avoid our friendly demons," Balthazar said and laughed out loud.

"How is this funny? Demons and betrayal. I can think of better jokes," Eran said angrily.

Billy was eager to tell them the rest of what had happened as he started to feel a pain in his head where he was kicked. "Balthazar, I met a paralytic man on our first trip to Capernaum. Do you remember? He was the one by the synagogue who told us about Jesus heading to Cana before we encountered our first creature."

"Of course. What of him? Did you see him again?"

"I did. He was standing and arguing with Judas at the Jerusalem temple. He saw me and spoke to me about Jesus and told me that Jesus had been performing several miracles since I left the trail looking for him. One miracle was healing his lame limbs. Another miracle happened recently. Jesus raised a dead man from the grave—literally from a grave in which he had been placed for dead," said Billy.

"Jehovah! I met this man. His name is Lazarus. He is the brother of one of Jesus's closest friends, Mary. Many came from miles away to see him and speak to him. He is the one resurrected by Jesus. An amazing miracle that has brought many souls to follow the Son of God. I followed Jesus here after meeting with him," said Balthazar.

Balthazar continued to clean off Billy's face. There was initially a lot of blood. Billy suddenly started picking up on a horrible smell and realized where they were. They were in the city dump. The creature must have dragged him there after he was knocked out.

"You have stopped bleeding. You have a large gash in the back of your head, and your right eye is marked with a significant bruise. You should be all right however," said Balthazar. "Now what happened after you met with the paralytic man?"

"He helped me spot Judas. I then followed Judas into the temple where I found him meeting with church officials. As the creature said, the power of Satan had influenced him, and he was plotting to betray Jesus in the Garden of Gethsemane. I hid behind a door and followed Judas into the street from the temple. As I pursued him, the creature we saw in the street attacked me. I hit my head on the wall of a building and was momentarily knocked out. I awoke to the creature standing over me. He told me I would not be able to interfere with Judas and that the plot was already in motion. He then kicked me in the head. His initial blow hurt me, but did not knock me out. He started dragging me here when I came to my senses and tried to resist. He kicked me in the head a second time and I blacked out," said Billy. "You would be proud of me though my friend. I stood up to it in the street and was able to drive it away without you or a talisman!"

"Your faith has grown since you have been here. And it seems your friendships as well. I found this one looking for you. He said you asked him to stay behind as you went to find out more about Judas," said Balthazar.

"I obeyed your wishes, Billy, but I had a strange feeling—a sense that something bad had happened to you. I came looking for you, ran into Balthazar, and we found you here after hearing from some men who had seen you here. They thought you were dead," said Eran.

"It is Wednesday, right?" Billy asked, knowing it was, but his head was pounding, and he wanted reassurance that he was not missing something.

"Today is Wednesday," Eran and Balthazar said simultaneously.

"I heard Judas and the church officials talking. Jesus and his closest disciples are having a meal tomorrow night. I did not hear where they are meeting, but afterward Jesus plans to head to the Garden of Gethsemane to pray. It is there that Judas plans to betray Jesus, and it is there where we will find him. We know where he will be; we just need to sit and watch for him."

"Billy, the garden is large. You will need all of us to keep watch in different parts of the garden so you don't miss him," said Eran.

Billy was again concerned for his friends. Eran was right, however. The garden was too large for Billy to cover all of it and find Jesus. They would need to work together. Helping Billy to his feet, the men went to Eran's house to plan for Thursday.

CHAPTER 16

GETHSEMANE

Billy, Eran, and Balthazar woke early on Thursday. Eran prepared breakfast as the three men were up before the children or Anna. Anna was pleased to have Eran make breakfast for the men and the family. Eran was a fine cook. The men spoke about their plans for later.

"If we all get to the garden as the sun is setting, we can fan out and look for signs of Jesus and his disciples. If they are not in the garden, we can take positions that allow us to see most of the garden and still see each other so we can communicate with our hands," said Balthazar.

"The garden can be very dark at night, but if we can position ourselves correctly we may be able to use some common light from torches," said Eran.

"I don't know if torches are a good idea. The situation with Judas and the church leaders makes me feel like we should use caution," said Billy.

"I agree with you both. Eran, there may be some common torches already burning in the garden that we can position ourselves by to use them. I also think Billy is right regarding the situation, and we should be very careful as to not draw unwanted attention from the church leaders or any Roman influence."

As the men ate their breakfast and discussed that night's possibilities, Billy felt compelled to tell the two men more about what he knew from history about Jesus. It was a moment in which he could not remember if he had told them that Jesus ultimately would be crucified. He feared he had not. He spoke so much to them both about finding him and had discussed some of the history from the Bible with Eran and perhaps at times with Balthazar. But he found himself backed into a corner, as he was about to put these men in jeopardy.

Ultimately, Jesus would be arrested that night. Judas was to betray him. Regardless of Judas and the money he took from the church officials, they would find Jesus, arrest him, and kill him. Jesus and the positive message he was sending as he traveled throughout Israel, combined with the miracles he was performing, took power away from the church officials, and rather than accept that he was the true Son of God, they were influenced by Satan with greed and wanted to eliminate him.

"Eran and Balthazar, I want to tell you both something that is very important. Tonight's efforts will not result in a positive outcome. You know I am from the future. I don't believe I have spoken to the two of you about what happens to Jesus. I fear I forgot to tell you, or as it happens sometimes, I failed to tell you because I was more worried about meeting Jesus and not what actually happens to him."

"What is it, Billy?" said Eran.

"I told you that we know he will be at a dinner and in Gethsemane tonight. We know that because of what I overheard Judas and the church officials discussing. I remember some of that from what I learned at church as a kid, but I did not remember some of it until I heard Judas and the other men say it. Well, there is something every person who follows Jesus's teachings knows in my time. Those who follow Jesus are called Christians. Many of them wear crosses—jewelry to remind them of Jesus and his sacrifice."

"I know where this is leading," said Balthazar.

"I don't. What is going on, Billy?" Eran said, confused.

"Eran, after Jesus is arrested in the Garden of Gethsemane, he is taken before Roman, Israeli, and local officials and is condemned to be crucified. As a matter of fact, it happens quickly. By this time tomorrow, Jesus will be tried and killed."

Billy allowed the information to sink into both men's thoughts. Billy was still fearful the two men would be angry. He looked at both and asked them to say something about what he had just told them, but both men said nothing. Billy feared they were speechless and would think less of him.

"Gentlemen, I apologize I did not tell you what was ultimately to happen in this story. I had the information in my head and was so concerned with my own mission to meet Jesus that I forgot to tell you this important part of the story. Please forgive me for being so selfish and foolish. The two of you deserved to know this before this moment, but certainly before you risk your lives and families. Deep down, I assumed I would be dealing with this by myself. I didn't know if I would see you again, Balthazar and Eran, I thought that when I said goodbye I would never see you again."

"We have been risking our lives since we began this journey, Billy. Since we met, you have never been alone in this endeavor. You are my friend. Eran is your friend. We will help you. My family knows the risk I have taken by coming to this country to find Jesus. This is my duty and my birthright. If I fall looking for Jesus, they will understand. They will be heartbroken, but it is something they accepted as I walked out the door. My father and my grandfather did the same before me. Eran, your situation is different. You have a wife and small children. This is not your birthright. I believe Billy and I should go alone," Balthazar said.

"I cannot believe you have said these things to me. I am hurt that you would try to exclude me from the opportunity to meet the Son of God because of a little risk. No, I am not an accomplished wise man or a man from the future. I am a lowborn apprentice to a blacksmith. But does my position in this world make me less worthy to seek someone who has performed miracles in the name of God? No. I am worthy because I believe. I can't buy sacrifices and give as much money as others at the temple, but I believe, and my faith is rich and expensive. But more than this, I am rich in friendship. Before you arrived, Billy, I was low and hurt. I blamed God for my brother's death. You came here with a positive light. You made me believe again. You cannot deny me the chance to fulfill my faith with Jesus."

Anna interrupted Eran. "If my husband wants to go with you, I will not stop him. You have my blessing to go, Husband. Find Jesus and help your friends. If something happens, and I pray it doesn't, you will be missed, but the situation is bigger than all of you. A moment with the Son of God is worth the risk. Jesus is worth the risk."

Billy was amazed by their responses. He feared they would be cross with him for excluding information from them. Eran and Balthazar reaffirmed a true friendship, and Anna reinforced the validity of their mission. She was a strong person. They would go together to the Garden that evening and find Jesus as one. An optimism filled the room, and they all took each other by their arms, including Anna, and they clinched their hands tightly. They had never been closer, and they had never been more convinced that their plan would succeed.

The men went to work that day early again. They talked to Tehan and explained to him that they wished to leave early again and that Balthazar would help where he could to make sure enough work was accomplished in order to make that happen. The head blacksmith accepted the terms of their offer, and they went to work. Balthazar, who knew very little about being a blacksmith, was put in charge of the bellows. It was his job to let the fire and furnace breath. It was a hard job in the heat—not that swinging a hammer, finishing, or creating metal pieces was any less difficult. Balthazar liked the work. It was simple, hard work.

"I am not sure I would want to do this every day, but for today this is a job I could repeat all day."

"You will do this most of the day, but you will also need to put wood and coal in the fire as well. As you add breath to the fire, you will burn the source of the fire and will need to replenish it. Keep an eye on it," said Eran.

"Yes sir!"

Billy chuckled at their banter. The day went by quickly, as there was much work to do, and all their hearts were light. They finished their work and left with the blessing of the head blacksmith. Balthazar, who was a fit man, complained a little about his fatigue and soreness, but admitted it was a good feeling. He felt good that he had put in an honest day's work.

The men stopped by Eran's to quickly clean up, eat, and get some supplies for the night. Balthazar and Billy stepped outside so Eran could say goodbye to Anna. They spoke to each other softly and both emerged with smiles—one ready for an adventure and the other ready to send off her love. Balthazar and Billy tried to say goodbye with words, but Anna took both in her arms by opening them as wide as possible. She held them for a few brief moments. Balthazar began to pull away but was pulled back in by Anna.

Anna then pushed them both away and said, "Make sure you look out for Eran. Look out for each other."

The men arrived at the Mount of Olives as the sun was beginning to set. The Garden of Gethsemane was located there just opposite and west of the temple. The city was quiet on the west side that night. Families gathered for the feast of Passover just as Jesus and his disciples were congregated to do the same. This was a celebration, but one held with reverence. Balthazar being a magi also noted the streets were quiet, almost as if the energy of the city were in a fog because of what was about to happen.

Balthazar said, "This city knows and loves Jesus. It feels the stress of the near future."

Billy said, "Do you mean the people or the city itself,"

"When a place has many people, like Jerusalem, it becomes alive with its own life and energy. The city itself feels the bend in the aura surrounding what is to come. The people may not even know."

The men looked throughout Gethsemane and did not find Jesus or his disciples anywhere. Logically, the group would be coming from the city, where they had their Passover dinner. The three positioned themselves where there was adequate lighting and a good view of anyone who would come into the garden from the city gates.

Eran found a tree where he could see above some of the hilly terrain and could clearly see the walls of Jerusalem. Balthazar was directly across from him in an area that was more topically flat but well lit by torches. Billy was furthest away from Eran and north of Balthazar. With the area they covered, it would be difficult to miss anyone coming from the city into that area.

Time passed slowly for the men eager with the anticipation of Jesus's arrival. Unlike the day where they felt like their work time was cut in half because they were looking forward to their opportunity to meet Jesus, this night proved to be the exact opposite. The three men stayed diligent, however. Before long, Billy was the first to see a group approaching. The group looked like they could be Jesus and his entourage.

Billy had a hard time seeing, as the garden had become darker as the evening progressed. He could not make out the group but could tell it was certainly people headed his way. Balthazar could no longer see Billy or Eran, and he did not see the group approaching Billy. Eran could see everything. He saw that the group approaching was not Jesus and his disciples.

The group were soldiers.

He quickly jumped down from his perch and ran to Balthazar. Before Eran could get to Balthazar, the group of soldiers had descended upon Billy. As Eran urged Balthazar to follow him, they got close enough to hear what was being said but stayed out of sight, in case there was trouble. The three men could not fight their way out of the situation if it became violent. Balthazar held off Eran, who would have rushed in to help. Balthazar remembered their earlier discussions and the words of Anna. He was not going to let Eran do something rash.

The leader of the soldiers said, "We have been looking for you. Put him in iron."

"What am I being arrested for," asked Billy.

"When you rob and steal from pilgrims as much as you have, how can you ask that question?"

"I think you have me confused with another person. My name is Billy. I am an apprentice to a blacksmith in Jerusalem. I have never robbed or murdered anyone," declared Billy.

"You can tell that to the prefect."

As the soldiers took Billy away, Balthazar watched helplessly while at the same time restraining Eran. Eran finally gave up fighting Balthazar, who was much bigger and stronger than he was. Eran threw Balthazar off him, but he did not go after Billy as the soldiers took him away. Sad and despondent, the two took a moment to gather their thoughts. Eran sat on the ground and crossed his arms over his bent legs and lowered his head into them. Balthazar stayed standing, watching Billy being led away.

"Did that just happen?" said Eran.

"That just happened," said Balthazar. "Billy and I followed Jesus throughout Israel. We were all the way to Tyre, Samaria, and here in Judea. When we separated, and he came to live with you, I went everywhere looking for him, and it was always the same situation every time. Some unforeseen force stopped us or me from finding Jesus. We had always missed him by minutes, hours, or days. It was frustrating, and it challenges one's faith. You must stay strong, Eran. The challenge is what makes it special, though it is very difficult. God himself has laid the very brick that makes the road that Billy is traveling on. Remember that God would not have brought Billy here without a divine plan. We must have faith in this regardless of our frustration and fear. If we give into the fear and the anger associated with this situation, we give strength to those who would bring evil to this earth. We can't—" Balthazar stopped speaking midsentence.

As the soldiers ushered Billy away and headed toward one of Jerusalem's eastern gates, a demon was spotted near a tree. One of the world's bringers of evil raised up from his lower position at the base of the tree and erected his wicked bent body up so Billy could see him as they took him toward Jerusalem.

The creature wanted Billy to know he was the playwright in this staged display of the soldiers, and as Billy walked passed him, he laughed with a malevolent tone only a dark entity could conjure. The creature's evil work was done. Billy was arrested and could not stop Judas or speak to Jesus. The wicked creature looked paler than the others, perhaps from his successful win over Billy.

Unfortunately for the men, as they watched helplessly as their friend was taken off by the soldiers, another group of men quietly slipped through the garden unnoticed behind them. They followed the group of soldiers to the eastern wall of the city. A gate opened, then Billy and his unwanted entourage went through, and the gate closed behind them.

The creature, now realizing Balthazar was angry and coming toward him, quickly turned and ran in the direction of the city. Then it stopped and turned back toward Balthazar and Eran. Eran, unable to control his emotions, let loose his anger. He picked up a stone and threw it at the creature. Eran recognized the evil entity as the same thing that confronted Billy in the street the other day. It had become even more powerful.

"We are not afraid of you," Eran said, remembering what Balthazar and Billy said about how their power grows.

"I am one of the fallen. Baptized in fire and darkness. You and your kind will always be afraid of me. My presence reminds you of your fall. We fell first, but you fell because of our influence. The world is influenced by us and our leader as much as it is influenced by God. Did you think your kind was safe? No!" shouted the creature.

"You have influence, but not greater than the influence of God. Good and evil will always be at odds, as it keeps things in balance. But in the end, those on the good side, God's side, will defeat evil.

You know this is true. This is what you fear. There are times your kind may win a few small battles against good and you and your master may feel comfortable, but it is the light of God and his love that are the most powerful influence in this world. You know it to be true, and each person who feels his love is what makes you weaker. You and your kind feel this as Jesus has made his way through Israel. Why else would you be so adamant about trying to stop Billy?" said Balthazar.

The creature said nothing but coughed and grunted like an angry dog that had a bone taken away from it. Balthazar was not an average human. He had been trained to be reasonable and logical. He had studied good and evil. He studied life and death. He and those before him in his family waited for the arrival of Jesus. His grandfather witnessed the wonder of his arrival many years ago and that brought confidence to all those touched by the news.

Balthazar's words were as strong as an incantation against the creature, and now it did not know what to do. As Balthazar said, the demon had won a small battle that moment by getting Billy arrested, but down deep the creature was aware that God's plans would be difficult to vanquish, even if Judas succeeded.

Balthazar motioned for Eran to move away from the creature. There were no more words to be exchanged between the two opposing sides. The two remaining men from the original party looked around the area. Seeing no one, they decided to stay together and stand watch. They assumed that anyone coming into the garden now would have torches to guide their way. They would sit together and keep vigil.

Balthazar and Eran sat together for a long time, waiting for any movement, not knowing that while they spoke to the creature, Jesus and his disciples had passed by them. While they faced the creature, a long distance behind them, the group walked passed them. Unknowingly, they sat watching and waiting patiently. The side of evil had won another small battle. The creature intentionally engaged with them to divert them, and those moments that lacked focus resulted in a win for the dark side.

After hours had passed, the men broke their silent vigil. Balthazar feared they had missed their quarry. Eran who was much younger and lacked patience, worried much sooner that something was wrong, and they may have not seen Jesus and his friends enter the garden.

"Balthazar, we have been waiting a long time. Do you think we missed them coming into the garden?" said Eran.

"I am concerned you are right."

As they spoke, the two of them saw lights in the distance moving across the area where Eran was originally positioned. Several torches moved across the garden. They were moving quickly. Billy and Eran stood up and ran toward the lights.

Once they were close enough, they could see that the lights were not Jesus and his men. They were a group of chief priests and officials from the temple with some soldiers or men of authority. They were carrying clubs, swords, torches, and other weapons. They moved quickly for a reason. They were closing in on their prey. As Balthazar and Eran followed them, they saw who the group of men were after. It was Jesus and a small group of his disciples.

"It must be Jesus. I have only seen him from a distance, but he is the Son of God," said Balthazar.

Jesus was kneeling in prayer as the men with weapons approached. Jesus and the men with him stood up. A man familiar with Jesus stepped up to him.

"Rabbi," the man said as he kissed Jesus directly on the cheek.

The other men in the group with the weapons pushed Jesus's men aside. They took a hold of Jesus. Jesus said something to his captors. Eran and Balthazar were unable to understand what he said. Jesus did not speak as loudly or distinctly as the man who said rabbi.

Perhaps Jesus was saddened by the betrayal or maybe the man who said rabbi was making sure the others received a special signal to take him. Jesus was then ushered away from where he was praying. Another small battle won by evil.

CHAPTER 17

PILATE

Billy was brought to the western part of the city into an opulent building. The influence of the Roman world was obvious in the architecture and landscape. Billy was reminded of the movies he had seen in the past, like *Spartacus* and *Ben Hur*. He remembered the ordered Cyprus trees and urns outside the homes of Roman officials. Roman soldiers or centurions stood guard at every doorway he passed, dragged along in chains by the men who arrested him.

Before him was a man sitting on a lavish and magnificent chair. It was not a throne, but it was adorned with precious metals and made of crafted marble. If the chair was a representation of the man's position and power, he was before someone who was important. The man had some paper in his right hand, and as Billy was brought before him, the man motioned for the soldiers to let go of him.

The men threw Billy down to his knees. Assuming he was in front of someone of rank, he stayed down there. A man who was lavishly dressed stepped from the right side of the man and announced the man on the fine chair as Pontius Pilate, prefect of Jerusalem and the region. The man speaking was well dressed and held a long scepter. His hair was gray and wavy. He had a gold ring on top of his head. Billy remembered the name of Pontius Pilate from Sunday school. He was in trouble.

"His Grace, Pontius Pilate, will now hear the case of Dismas," said the man with the scepter.

"Dismas, you have been accused of robbery, assault, and murder in the regions of Samaria, Galilee, Tyre, Ulatha, and Gaulanitis. Though many of your crimes have been committed in regions outside my jurisdiction, your wrongdoings have been taken into account as detrimental to the entire geographic area and therefore are subject to Roman law as any other criminal. What say you to these charges?" said Pilate.

One of the soldiers kicked Billy when he did not respond right away. He was cast upon the floor, his hands sprawling on the ground, stopping his body from completely being thrown, parallel to the cold floor. Billy looked back at the soldier with a scowl. The soldier raised his right arm with a kind of a small whip in his hand.

The soldier had a scowl on his face. The soldier had a general distaste and hatred for all criminals, but especially those who showed any resistance. When Billy turned and showed his emotions, it was an open invitation for the soldier to add pain and suffering to an already volatile situation.

"Enough," shouted Pilate, having experienced this soldier's anger and spite before. "What do you have to say, Dimas?"

Billy hurt from the kick to the back by the soldier. Wincing, he used his hands to rise back to his knees from all fours. The pain was acute. The soldier had kicked him in his left kidney. Billy was much thinner than he was at the beginning of his journey. The food he ate in Israel in this period, combined with walking everywhere for travel, made him thinner. His lazier self would not have been injured by the kick. His fat would have blocked the blow.

"I did not respond to you, sir, because I do not recognize the name Dismas, Your Grace," Billy said, trying to gain favor.

"Are you trying to say you are not the criminal who Jewish and Roman authorities have been looking for years?" asked Pilate.

"That is exactly what I am saying, sir."

The soldier struck Billy with the butt of his small whip, where the neck and back meet. He was looking for an opportunity to strike Billy, and the few truthful words Billy uttered were enough. Pilate again showed his disgust in the soldier's actions and asked the soldier to stand down.

Pilate was still a young man. He had a full head of hair that was combed straight to his eyebrows. The bangs of his hair were slightly curled. He was dressed well. He was an average-size man of his time—not too tall and certainly not short. He was a good-looking man, whose looks were aided by his ability to have his hair perfected by someone other than himself and the money he was able to spend on his clothing.

He had full robes on that were off white. His clothing was stylized by a reddish cloak that draped over his off-white robes. He had a large gold leaf, like a gold crown, on his head. He looked bored sitting on his fancy chair and acted as if he wanted to be one hundred other places, rather than in the court and the hearing.

Every day was a laborious glimpse into the underworld of Jerusalem and the region to him, dealing with degenerates, liars, and thieves. One could tell he was young and rich and hoping this position would lead to another much easier and more prestigious opportunity. He acted as if he grew up in privilege and not from hard work. His disdain for those he handed verdicts on and disgust for those he worked with was clear. He did not want to be there, and his body language displayed his frustration with the situation.

Billy recognized his type from his younger days, when he was in his own time and place. His dad was always gracious to men and women like Pilate. His father would try and mentor those men and women to be more present in what they were involved with rather than always looking to what was next in the future. His father would tell Billy to be aware of possibilities that present themselves, but to always do his best with what he was currently doing.

A great example his father would use to show Billy what he

meant was related to the travel programs in their community. For basketball, there were several youth teams and organizations. His father would point out to Billy that there were several kids that played on three to four teams in many years. Their parents pulling them from one program and putting them in another. Many times, the reasoning for switching was slight. Sometimes there was a coach who did not offer enough playing time to the child or another program offered a discount or more opportunities.

There were times when parents would think the program or the coach were not using the player correctly, whether by position or plays, to score. Basically, Billy's father was saying the parents were impatient and looking for the next great thing for their son or daughter rather than developing the opportunity they already had.

To those parents and those men and women, the grass always seemed greener on the other side of the fence, as the old saying goes. Billy's father would say Pontius Pilate was one of those people. Bored with what he had and what he was doing, looking for the next chance rather than focusing on what was right in front of him. Billy did not feel comfortable with this kind of person judging him as prefect of the region.

"Sir, I am not this person you say I am. I have only been in the region for a while and have been living in the city for nearly a year. I am an apprentice in a blacksmith shop, not a thief and certainly not a murderer. My name is Billy, not Dismas. I have never even heard the name Dismas before today. I admit to traveling this region around the Sea of Galilee before coming to live here in Jerusalem, but I did not commit any crimes. I have not hurt anyone," said Billy.

"According to the charges, you were identified as Dismas by a man who said you attacked him outside of Capernaum. He was with our detail of soldiers in the garden and was able to pick you out immediately," said Pilate.

"Forgive me for saying so, Your Grace, but it was very dark in the garden tonight. This man who claims to know my identity has not seen me in the light. This room, for example, is lit by numerous lamps, and there would be an ample opportunity to see my face clearly here. I believe I should be allowed to face my accuser—that I may challenge his false charges and bring my innocence to light, literally," said Billy.

Billy thought about mentioning Balthazar and Eran in an attempt to improve his argument, but then he also thought his captors might arrest them as well, and he would put them and Eran's family in jeopardy. He could not tell Pilate about his exceptional circumstances either. No one would believe he was brought here to this time by God for a purpose that was still unclear. They would for sure find him guilty.

Crazy is not an attribute of the situation he was currently in. In Billy's time, criminals often claimed they were criminally insane when they committed crimes or atrocities. But here in Israel, during the time of Jesus, he was quite sure modern psychology would not be an answer to the charges. This world predated modern psychology by about eighteen hundred years. Billy was in serious trouble. He did not want to mention his friends and certainly not Jesus or the truth about his presence there.

"My soldiers trust the man well who has identified you. He has been working with us ever since he was attacked and left for dead. He has made it clear that you are the one who attacked him," said Pilate.

"What is his name that I may better know my accuser?"

"I have heard enough. This man before me is clearly lying. He has been identified as the murderer and thief Dismas and is sentenced to hang upon a cross until dead. This sentence will be carried out tomorrow morning. May there be mercy for you in the afterlife," Pilate said, bored with the situation and ready for the next criminal case.

"But I am not the man who has done these crimes. Please go to the head blacksmith I work for, and he will tell you that I have been busy working every day for him for a while now," Billy pleaded as he was abruptly brought to his feet and dragged back out of the impressive Roman building.

As he was forcibly being led out of the building, he lowered his head in frustration. He heard a voice that sounded peaceful and comforting. He struggled to raise his head as he was being manhandled by the soldiers.

"Billy. Billy, I will see you again. Do not give up hope," said Jesus as he was being brought in to Pontius Pilate.

Billy was speechless as the distance between him and Jesus grew, became closer, and then grew apart again. The door to the building shut, and as Billy tried to look back, Jesus slowly went out of sight as the door finally closed. The guard who sadistically kicked Billy was the one responsible for removing him, and he was taken out of the building and brought to a dark gate that was closed with large iron on the outside and a second gate made of wood on the inside that was reinforced further with thick iron pieces across every three feet to add strength.

This was a gate meant to keep people out or keep people in. Passed the gate, left and right, were thick and tall walls made of brick and mortar. They were too tall to penetrate unless one had a ladder or rope, and they were too thick to pummel through with any tools. There were hardly any windows or openings anywhere in the structure that he could see.

Men stood guard on top of the immense walls. This was a place for criminals. Billy realized he was being locked away until he would be killed on the cross. A deep sadness filled Billy's heart. So many times he was so close to meeting Jesus, and now all hope was lost, as he was going to die on the cross. He drew some solace from having seen Jesus and heard his words of encouragement.

Meanwhile, back in the opulent building, Jesus's trial with Pontius Pilate was about to begin. Again, as with Billy, Pilate looked at the information given to him about Jesus and angrily lowered his right hand with the paper containing information about Jesus to his knee. Pilate, being an impatient man, raised up to speak.

"This man has been accused and convicted by his own people of religious crimes against the Jewish church. The officials who have signed these papers have adequately provided enough information regarding this case to have convicted this man for heresy in their own hearing. Since this man is from Galilee, Herod Antipas, the ruler of this city and region, should hear the case and he be brought before him immediately. As the Roman prefect and procurator of this city and region, I do not consider myself the correct official to judge this man and render a final verdict. Let him be taken before Herod Antipas with the documentation from the Sanhedrin. Let the word of the Jewish officials be shown to Herod and let him sit in judgment on this man," said Pilate, who washed his hands in a tall basin filled with water and rose petals close to his fantastic chair.

Pontius Pilate motioned for the soldiers to take Jesus away. Pilate told everyone present that he would hear no more cases. Pilate went to rest. He assumed the transfer of the prisoner Jesus would be quick and painless, as he was operating court out of Herod's palace, which would explain the beautiful building that Billy had seen.

The soldiers took Jesus but had to pause, as one of the soldiers went to find out where they could find Herod Antipas. Billy was not to be tried by Herod, as he was thought to be criminal at large for thievery and murder in the region. Such crimes fell under the jurisdiction of Pontius Pilate. Jesus was Jewish and being accused of treason and heresy by Jewish church officials.

Pilate himself admitted he needed to be seen by Herod in order to be condemned by local law. Unfortunately, Herod Antipas was not in his palace. Since Pilate came to judge in the area, Herod set him up in his palace and then went to celebrate the feast of Passover in the western palace, which was close to his own.

"Herod isn't here," said the soldier who went to find Herod in the building.

"What? Well, where is he? Get Pontius Pilate back here so he can claim this case and get this man processed," said the ranking officer.

Pilate was nowhere to be found, however. When the soldiers went to get him, they were told he was indisposed. They would have to find Herod and take Jesus before him now. The men were frustrated. That night they arrested Jesus in the Garden of Gethsemane after Judas betrayed him with a kiss. They then took Jesus before the high priest Calaphas and then before the Jewish Sanhedrin. Many of the men of the Sanhedrin were the same who met with Judas; they planned and executed Jesus's arrest.

There was very little need for the hearings in front of Caliphas and the Sanhedrin. The verdict of both Caliphas and the Sanhedrin was easily reached. They wanted to eliminate Jesus. He was in their way. He challenged their authority and the way that they went about their business of faith. Jesus sought truth and wanted the people to hear it, while the church officials wanted the people to compliantly follow their teachings. Jesus challenged those teachings and made himself a threat.

After Jesus met with Caliphas and then was taken before the Sanhedrin, Jesus was brought before Pontius Pilate. Pilate threw out the case saying there was no reason for him to rule on Jesus as the ruler of the territory. Since the accusations were more about faith than Roman law, Herod should be the one to preside.

The soldiers found out quickly where Herod Antipas went, and they quickly moved to get Jesus in front of him. Herod had been celebrating all night by the time Jesus was brought before him. Herod was not a pious man but was celebrating, as it was an opportunity to exercise excess.

He was known to be a cruel and stern ruler. He was even more so when intoxicated. Herod was not hospitable to Jesus. He had heard of Jesus and John the Baptist. He did not like how popular the two men were to the people of the region. Herod thought that if he ordered the death of Jesus, the people might revolt, angry that he killed their leader, much like the situation with John the Baptist. Herod thought of ways to catch Jesus in a trap that would give him a clear way to kill him without the people getting angry.

"You are the messiah, the chosen one to lead Israel out of darkness?" asked Herod.

"I am," said Jesus calmly.

For quite some time, Herod asked Jesus questions. He was frustrated by Jesus's tranquil responses. Herod could not get him flustered. Herod then asked Jesus to perform a miracle in front of him. Jesus refused him, knowing what part he was to play in the situation. Herod could not get Jesus to say or do anything that would make condemning him to death any easier. Frustrated with Jesus's peaceful approach to his attempts to catch him in a lie or to say something that would appease the masses, he was unrighteous and wanted to get back to his celebration. Herod ordered that he be brought back to Pontius Pilate.

Before Jesus was returned to Pilate, Herod allowed his soldiers to torture Jesus. The soldiers were harsh. They stripped Jesus of his clothes and covered him in adorning royal attire. A few of the men made a crown of thorns, and they put it on Jesus's head. Blood came from the spots where the thorns pushed into Jesus's scalp.

It was very early morning when Jesus was brought back to Pontius Pilate. Jesus was a sorry sight to see. Bleeding from the crown of thorns and dirtied from his treatment, he was covered in dust and dirt from being pushed down.

A crowd had begun to congregate outside of Herod's palace. News that Jesus was arrested and being tried had spread through the city. As with many cultures, many of the same people who praised Jesus's entrance into the city a few days earlier were now calling for his conviction. The city of Jerusalem loved a winner when it was easy to support them, but they loved a loser even more when that person was down.

Pontius Pilate, tired from the earlier proceedings, came out to address the unruly crowd. He asked them what they wanted. Several of the demon creatures were in the crowd. Influenced by the creatures as they shouted out angry and evil words about Jesus, the crowd worked themselves into a frenzy.

There was another prisoner who had committed much greater crimes than Jesus there at the same time. Pilate asked the crowd if they would like to pardon Jesus or the other prisoner. Strangely, the crowd called for the conviction and crucifixion of Jesus rather than the other prisoner. Evil would win this small battle again as the creatures led the shouts to crucify Jesus.

Pilate wanted to appease the crowd. He knew that Jesus was innocent and did not deserve to be condemned. The other prisoner was deplorable and should have been the one to die, but the crowd wanted Jesus to be crucified. Going against what he knew to be right, as he was not strong enough to challenge the crowd, Pilate convicted Jesus of the false charges against him and had the soldiers take him to prison, where he would be held until crucified.

CHAPTER 18

The Final Road

It was very early in the morning. One could feel how early it was, as there was a slight chill in the air that came from the sun being hidden on the other side of the world all night, with the moon only providing light and not heat through the darkness. The quiet in the jail and specifically the cell Billy was in was another tip that no one was moving other than Billy.

He was awakened by the chill. He slept on a pile of straw in the corner of the cell. No blanket or comfort was provided. Not even a rug to put on the floor or over the hay was awarded. He was a criminal in the eyes of his captors and was treated as such. A small amount of light began to creep in to the cell from the small window just above him. His window must be facing the east.

Billy jumped up, and with his fingers he grabbed the edge of the windowsill. He pulled himself up with his arms and put his feet on the wall to brace himself. He looked out and saw the sun beginning to rise over the buildings of Jerusalem. There was great beauty in this particular sunrise. Billy saw the blessing of the sun on the day his captors would be carrying out the death sentence on him.

Billy could hear feet moving over the hard floors outside the cell. Keys jingled on a jailer's hip as he walked down the hallway of the jail, making sure all was secure and nothing happened during the night. The jailer stopped and looked in on Billy and continued to do so at each cell. He said nothing to Billy or any of the other prisoners. He simply checked that the prisoners were still in the cells and had not tried to commit suicide during the night.

Billy heard the same jailer and another guard discussing it the night before. The jailer told the other guard that the only job they had to do before handing over the prisoners was to make sure they had not killed themselves during the night. Billy imagined that a lonely night for some people would cause them to contemplate very dark thoughts.

As Billy lay on the cold floor and straw, he woke up several times during the short night as his mind investigated the end of his life in a foreign place and time. He did not sleep well and thought back to when his life was much simpler.

Billy thought about his Saturdays and Sundays when he was a different man so long ago. He would sleep until noon at times. His wife would get up and make breakfast, go for a walk, attend church, or visit the grocery store or run other errands before he ever thought of making it down to the couch, where he would watch TV and eat all day. He never changed his routine and hoped his family would have their own agendas on those days so he would be alone to do nothing. No one to bother him—no problem.

His wife would open the drapes when she woke to stir him, but he would close them when she was on her way. She had to take care of getting the kids to their games, school, and other activities. He did not attend many games. Billy hardly went to anything. His family expected nothing less from him. The strange thing was, Billy did not relish his bankrupt soul or lazy days as he looked out into the hall, watching the jailer checking each prisoner. He longed for another chance to be better.

Billy asked the jailer, "Are we to be fed this morning?"

"No! We are not going to waste good food on condemned men," he said.

Billy was very hungry and still cold. The beginning warmth of the morning sun now aggressively filled the cell and other parts of the jail, but still had not warmed everything it touched. The jailer yelled something angrily at another prisoner and whipped his hands that were protruding from the opening in the jail cell door. The man quickly withdrew his hands and let out a yell that combined pain and sadness. Truly the men in the jail were desperate and unfortunate. Billy was one of them.

In order to keep his mind off the impending doom he faced, Billy took an inventory of his family. He began with his children. He thought of their faces. He imagined them smiling and happy to see him. He could feel the warmth of the sun coming from behind him through the window in the cell. As he daydreamed of his children, his core body temperature warmed. It was unclear if it was the spiritually warm thought of his children or the warmth of the sun that was the reason for the change in his body temperature, but he was feeling much better.

Billy then dreamed of his wife. He imagined kissing her on her thin lips while running his hands up and down her back. She stepped back, still being held in his arms, and smiled at him. She had a look on her face of pure contentment and mirth. He took her by her hands and was beginning to tell her how he felt about her.

Billy told her how beautiful she was and how no other woman had ever made him feel the way she did. He told her how he appreciated all she did for him and for the children and how she deserved to be treated as if it were Mother's Day every day. Not the kind of Mother's Day where he picked up a card and a crappy gift from the Walgreen's drugstore because it was the closest store and the only one open at that time because he was late to shop.

He meant the kind of Mother's Day in which she would open a homemade coupon book with coupons for a free back rub, a coupon for a free foot massage, a coupon for a candlelit dinner, and many more. He had flowers for her from the specialty florist who was an artist in college, but now applied her talents and eye for color to her arrangements.

She had mentioned the florist a million times, but he never purchased anything from her because he was not actually listening. Billy was daydreaming himself a better husband and she loved everything he was doing. Just then the jail door opened, and he was being ushered into the hallway. It was time.

As cold as Billy was in that early part of the morning, he was wishing for the cool air to return. As he and the other men walked out of the jail and into the courtyard outside, the sun was already challenging. Without sandals or shoes, he could feel the sharp, tiny stones beneath his feet. The guards directed the men toward a pile of wood. Billy recognized what the wood was when he got closer to the pile.

He was looking at crosses.

Billy's heart sank into his stomach. A dark reality hit him as the sun brightly shown down on the pile of crosses. One of the guards snapped a whip and screamed at the men to get things moving. He saw several other men go to the pile, pick up the heavy wood, and place the crutch of the cross on their shoulders. The weight was significant.

He saw a strong-looking man wince and nearly fall as he loaded the wood construct onto his shoulder and back. Billy was next in line. Remembering advice from coaches when he was a young athlete, Billy squatted down and used his legs more than his back to lift his cross. His cross was not on the ground, but one of the three crosses up and raised.

Billy said a small prayer for the cross being off the ground as he saw other men struggle to raise their crosses from the bare ground. One man could not lift his cross. Billy tried to balance his on the ground and give him a hand at the same time. The guards disapproved and snapped their whips. The crackling sound of the whips was enough motivation for the weak, condemned men, and he was one of them. With great labor, he raised the cross from the ground. With a tremendous amount of exertion, he joined the others.

The men were lined up and given instructions. The jailers and guards were cruel men. They dealt with hard men who were criminals, so they had forgotten empathy and graciousness. As Billy listened to them, he thanked God for his strange opportunity to change.

He was not the man he was on the day of his birthday so long ago. He was not on the couch. He had traveled the world of Christ and been to Jerusalem. He had survived a leopard and demons. These men were sad beings. Billy pitied them. He felt a peculiar compassion for all of them, and he prayed God would allow them a chance to see the light of goodness—that they would transform and change as he had done.

"Dear Lord, these men have been made callus by their profession. Each day they usher evil men to their doom. They administer justice at the hand of their government and see very little positivity. Please allow them the same chance for change that I was given. Please give them a simple opportunity to find your love so that the burden of their jobs may be lightened," Billy prayed.

"You will stay in formation as we travel. If you fall for any reason, we will remind you why you need to keep on your feet. Believe me when I say we will remind you strongly. You will keep your feet. You are all condemned men. Your lives are forfeit. You still have a job to do for Jerusalem, however.

"Your job is to make the young men who see you pray they never break the law under our government. You will make all those who see you weep over the prospect of being convicted. You will want to fall and give up as you carry your cross to where you will ultimately perish. Do not falter. Remember that the harder you work to get to the drop of your cross, the easier it will be for you to lose consciousness when you are on the cross and enter the afterlife. This will be challenging for you, but imagine it as a small penance for your crimes. If there is mercy, you will die quickly. Wherever your god or gods take you, it will be quicker—it will be with less torment on the cross," said the lead jailer.

The lead jailer cracked his whip with his right hand, and with a violent motion of his left he moved the group toward the gate at the end of the jail's courtyard. Billy looked to find Jesus and could not see him. He did not see him as they initially entered the courtyard, and he could not find him now.

There was a good number of men there that morning. Each man was paying for his crime or misconduct. Billy was potentially the only man there who was not guilty of a wrongdoing. Billy reassured himself that there was a possibility of seeing Jesus before or when they arrived at the place they were to be crucified.

The lead jailer had told them that there were numerous places where the crosses were erected with the criminals on them. All the men made their way toward their end. Billy accepted the possibility that he may not see Jesus again. It lowered his heart, and he struggled to come to grips with that reality. As a new man changed by his experiences and enduring so much during Jesus's time, he was disappointed. His time with Balthazar and the other people he had experienced there made him positive and optimistic. He was no longer the dark, brooding man on the couch. But as he looked at the difficult prospect of being executed on a cross without meeting Jesus, he found the situation desperate and disheartening.

The men paused while their captors opened the jail's courtyard gate. In the brief intermission of their trip toward their end, Billy looked at the shadow cast from the sun through the man in front of him. The man's body combined with the cross on his back and shoulders, with the position of the gate and the archway holding it, cast a shadow that looked like an angel at the gate of heaven.

As the man in front of him moved slightly, it gave the appearance of the angel's hands reaching out to Billy. Billy closed his eyes and imagined the angel's arms engulfing him and the wings of the angel shielding him, protecting him. Billy was to be slaughtered on the cross. Having an angel take him into its wings gave him solace, regardless if the presence of Jesus was there or not.

The assembly of men made their way out of the jail and onto the street. Billy was not familiar with this part of Jerusalem. He spent most of his time on the other side of town while waiting for Jesus to arrive for his final days on earth. Billy lived closer to a garden called Gethsemane on the east side of the city.

He thought with fondness and gratefulness of Eran and his family. Eran's family had been very good to him, and Eran had helped him locate Jesus. He wished he was still living with them on the east side of the city, waiting for Jesus, when the daily moments, no matter how mundane, were filled with hope.

The task of carrying the cross proved difficult. The guards and jailers pushed the men by lashing out with their whips and by saying indiscernible phrases that had meaning because of the way they were said, unrelated to the harsh words that were spoken. After a short distance, the heat affected some of the men, and they began to veer off course.

Some needed to stop by the side of the road to regain their breath and strength. The sun pounded on the men, causing strain and tension. He did not know how long they had to go, but carrying the cross made the effort daunting. One of the men asked a captor how long they would have to travel and was beaten severely. When the man could not get up and go further, he was given a beating again, which prompted him to get up and try again to walk. He was in terrible pain.

Billy's feet hurt so badly. As he struggled to move the cross down the street, he looked down and realized they were bloody and leaving a footprint on the dust of the coarse street. He was in agony as he advanced. Many of the men were equally having a difficult time with the task at hand. There were a lot of bystanders on the side of the road. Some of those in the crowd were cruel and hurled insults at the condemned men who labored by them. Other members of the mob were less unkind and offered something to drink, wiped the brows of those who were sweating profusely, and one man took the cross from one of the prisoners who had fallen and could not continue.

The prisoner who could not continue had really been worked over by the guards. Billy noticed the blood on his face as he passed by, and the kind man from the crowd helped him with the cross. Billy realized something too late. He tried to stop and turn back but was violently attacked by the guards pushing the procession. The man who could not continue was Jesus! Billy tried to look back, but again the guards were harsh.

Billy cried out to God, "Why bring me here and give me the task of finding him only to fail so close to him? What am I here, if not to meet your son? What do you want of me?"

As he cried out to God, Billy felt the hard end of a whip come down just above his forehead. Before he went unconscious, he recognized that he unfortunately was hit with the scourge Tehan had made in the blacksmith shop. When he came to, blood was streaming down his face, and he could taste it. His face was filled wet with blood and sweat.

He could barely see, as the blood was stinging his eyes and blocked his vision. He could hear the familiar sound of the head jailer screaming. The head jailer had attacked him.

Billy stumbled up and onto his feet using his hands at first. He now looked down at the cross lying on the ground, stained with some of his blood. Billy was angry. He was mad at the jailer for hitting him. He was angry with God for the sad and disappointing situation. He was simply angry.

With anger and frustration, he lifted the heavy lumber shaped into a cross and raised it to his shoulder and back. He felt independent and charged with anger. He would make it to where the cross was to be risen and face death with no dread, despite what he thought would happen during his travels. He was momentarily focused on the place where he would end his life, when a gentle but clear voice reached his ears.

"Do not give up on your Lord," Jesus said as he and the man

helping him struggled by with the heavy cross on their shoulders. "Your journey here is not yet finished."

With his mouth open, Billy watched them pass by him. Jesus moved gracefully. His steps were full of purpose, and his fierce eyes locked with Billy's and did not leave him. A second pain hit Billy's head, this time on the backside. Billy dropped to the ground, and he passed out there on the street.

Jesus knew his thoughts and heart. Billy felt bad for giving up on God and Jesus. This moment showed how easily a situation could change one's emotions and feelings. Billy asked for forgiveness before being overcome by the jailer's blow.

CHAPTER 19

THE CROSS

Billy was awakened by cold water crashing on his face. Billy was looking into the sun but could tell that the silhouette of the man who threw the water on him was the lead jailer. Billy was lying down on his back, but he did not feel the hard pavement. He realized quickly that he was sprawled out in a strange fashion, and he was filled with tremendous pain.

The pain was much greater than before, when his feet were bleeding on the street. Billy realized what had transpired. He was no longer on his way to the cross; he was on it. Both his hands and feet were ablaze with aching agony. The cross lay on the ground. Someone must have carried him and the cross to this spot, and while he was unconscious he was placed on the cross and nailed to it.

"I woke you up so you could feel the true pain on the cross. It was the least I could do for you after you missed the journey here by passing out," the lead jailer said as he motioned to men holding ropes to raise the cross.

As the men pulled on the ropes, the bottom of the cross was positioned before a shallow narrow hole. Two other men nudged the bottom of the cross forward and it sunk into the hole with a thud. As the cross bounced, upon hitting the bottom of the hole, Billy felt a new intense and sharp pain as the weight of his body pulled at the nails where his hands and feet were pinned upon the cross.

Billy was now looking at his 180-degree view. Below him were several soldiers and jailers who had nailed him to the cross and raised him. There were a few people forming a crowd, but they were keeping their distance. Another small group of women were present. They seemed very upset. All of them were crying steadfastly. Billy assumed they were there for another prisoner who was to be crucified, as he did not recognize them.

The pain was intense. Billy agonized and tried to let his mind roam away from the cross. He used a familiar technique. He closed his eyes, trying not to let the pain overcome him. He imagined that his family was there in the crowd and they were concerned as they looked upon him. It made him feel better to know he would be mourned and that their love was present as he would slowly pass away.

As a child, Billy enjoyed feeling sad. It felt good to go to a dark place in his mind and think about his father's passing when young. He had similar feelings as he hung on the cross, pining over his family. He saw the face of his wife. She looked up at him with pity, but not like the pity she once had for his lowly state on the couch.

Her pity was no longer that of worry for him—it was pride and admiration. He was dying unfairly, and he pretended she knew it. Billy framed a scenario in which his wife and children knew of his travels and trials. They were proud that he had taken on the task of finding Jesus. His family was very religious, and in some peculiar way he wanted them to know of his newfound faith in God and Jesus. He imagined they were so pleased with him. Though they were not there, he spoke to them.

"I have so much to tell you. I have so much to say, and I don't know where to begin. First of all, I love you. Sarah. I have always loved you, even if I did not show it to you properly. Even if my actions were not that of one who loved you and the kids, the love was there. It was locked away in a dungeon of pain and despair.

I have learned much during my time in the holy land," Billy said imaginatively, only to be interrupted by the sound of a loud thump.

The loud thump was the sound of a second prisoner being risen to his place on the cross. Billy looked to his left and saw the man in suffering settle into position, hanging on the wood. Billy looked down from the man on the cross and noticed that there was one more shallow hole for a final cross. The other men who were in the painful procession must have been ushered to another location for their executions.

Billy wondered if they were to be executed in the same way or if there was a reason they were not all positioned together. He thought that maybe they were placed where they were for the severity of their crimes or maybe because of where they were from.

Nonetheless, there were only three holes to be filled by crosses on the hill that day, and two of them were already filled. The third hole remained unoccupied. There were many things to consider while hanging on a cross. Billy no longer preoccupied himself with the missing criminal, and his mind wandered elsewhere again.

"Can you forgive me for the time I wasted?" he said to his wife as he daydreamed. "I've had many years to be the kind of husband and father you and the children deserve. I failed miserably, and though I am unable to make amends, I want you to know what I could have and should have been to you and the kids and the community. I should have taken time with each child to know and love them. I should have given the time to serve the community alongside the interests of our children. As a leader, as a coach, like my father. Not just for my children but for the entire community."

As Billy dreamed, another thud sunk into the ground. It was the final criminal. Billy could not see his face, as he was looking downward with his chin in his chest. This man was not in agony. He had momentarily passed out from being nailed to the cross. There was a lot of blood on his face, and he was unrecognizable. Billy thought that all the criminals must look similar: stripped bare of their clothes, bloodied by beatings, and dirty from the journey to the hill.

All of them were indiscernible criminals, unworthy in the eyes of those who were punishing them. A group of men finely dressed said cruel words and mocked the man on the middle cross. They looked as if they were officials, as they had robes on that looked to be ceremonial. They disgusted Billy. Here a man was already in anguish on the cross, dying a slow death, and there they were to add insults to his woes. Their actions were disrespectful and cowardly.

He soon recognized some of the men from the synagogue. They were the men who spoke to Judas. At that moment, Billy realized what was happening. During his pain from the crucifixion and his drifting in and out of a dream state, where he was speaking his final words to his wife, he did not realize who was on the cross next to him. Very slowly, he turned his head back to the left.

The criminal on the cross was no longer chin down. He was staring directly at Billy, with focused and alert eyes. He managed to crack a smile at Billy with some effort. Billy could tell it hurt him to look his way and show the painful emotion. It was Jesus on the cross next to him.

Billy had been from Capernaum to Cana and from Nazareth to Jerusalem, searching for him, and now he was dying right next to him. Billy wanted to speak with Jesus so badly during his long stretch there and had practiced and prepared what he might say numerous times, but now he was speechless and in awe of the Son of God before him to the left. Tears of joy poured from Billy's eyes. He was so sad that they were both in their predicament, but joyous that he was a witness to Jesus's final hours.

"You now have me all to yourself," said Jesus, struggling again to smile, but he did. "You have endured much during your time here. I can only imagine how your reality has been tested as you wandered my time and world. Your time is so much different than this one—modern machines, electricity, and so many people. This is a much simpler time. It is a simpler time but still filled with selfishness and greed. The periods are similar in that sense. There is so much chaos in this moment today. Look out upon the people present. You see the chief priests and officials in that group mocking me? They have come to see me finished. They do not feel the love of my Father. They are more concerned with making sure their will is influenced, their pockets are full of gold, and their stomachs are full of wine and food. I fear they may not feel the force of my Father's plan, but their children and their children will. Over there, my mother and some of my followers weep for me. They do not yet realize this is only one small part of what will happen. My death serves a much greater purpose than anyone can fathom here today. The sadness they feel is real, but it is wrong, for my death signals the beginning of the new world."

Billy admired the way Jesus approached his death and his amazing sense of all that was around him. He respected Jesus and could listen to him speak about any topic, even with his hands and feet nailed to a cross. Billy felt guilty that he called out to God in anger and frustration on the street. God was looking out for him, even when he thought he was forsaken. Selfishly, Billy sought answers. Why was he there? What was the purpose for John the Baptist to send him after Jesus if just to die on the cross next to him? Would his family be OK without him? There were so many topics that needed answering.

"Billy, have you ever seen a forest that was cleared? After the large trees are cut down, the plants that once lived under the trees die out. The plants that live under the canopies of the trees don't need a lot of sunlight, so when the trees are cleared, too much sunlight kills the plants that are sensitive to so much light. The animals and insects that lived among the plants die or move on as well," Jesus said as he winced in pain.

"What if only one tree was removed? What change would that have on the forest? Depending on the size of the tree, hundreds and maybe thousands of ground-floor plants would die from exposure to the sun. So it is with people. Some people are large trees, some are plants on the ground floor, and others are insects or animals. Each has their part to play in this world, but when you remove one of them, the impact may be large or small, but it does not go unnoticed. The seeds of the tree make sure that when only one large tree falls due to sickness, age, overgrowth, there is another that will grow up and take its place. This is how the forest replenishes itself."

Both men were in considerable pain as they conversed. The man to the far left of them was in terrible distress. He was breathing so loud and heavy to cure his pain it could be heard by all there. A few boys who should not have been there to witness such horror mimicked his breathing as they ran up to the crosses, as if dared, and then recoiled as the third man spit at them and cursed them. The boys lost their courage and did not return after being rebuked. The third man on the cross looked to his right at both Jesus and Billy.

"If you are truly the Son of God as they say, why you don't save yourself and us?" the man said.

"Do you not fear God? For he is the Son of God, and he is condemned like you and I, but he is not guilty of any crime," Billy said.

"Be still, Billy, and save your energy. Thank you for standing up for me, but this is my fate. I have been treated this way, so I suffer as I expected. Each horror inflicted upon me with action or words was known before it hurt my flesh or bruised my heart," said Jesus, lowering his head momentarily, grimacing from pain.

Billy was careful to say anything and felt ashamed of his outburst to the other criminal. Jesus was a model for graciousness. Jesus even asked his Father to forgive all of those who were doing wrong to him, saying they did not know what they were doing. Billy was a man who would get upset at his kids or his wife for disturbing him when he was so busy watching television on the couch.

Jesus was asking forgiveness to people who were mocking him and had assaulted him and put him on a cross. Billy inwardly asked Jesus's Father for forgiveness. Still slow and unaccustomed to praying, Billy's words to God came easily. His heart was free and open, and he was able to express himself clearly.

After he asked God for forgiveness, he looked to Jesus and said, "I am sorry for the time I have wasted on this earth and the sins I have committed that have added to your pain and suffering on the cross. I did not know the treasures I had in my life and how blessed I was until I was brought here. I am a different man today than I was many years ago before my journey to find you started."

"You heard my words about the many trees or one tree taken down or falling in the forest? Once removed, everything below will change. I have told you this parable for a reason. Your father, Billy, was a large tree to your family and your community. You were supposed to be the tree that replaced him. You allowed the sunlight to stunt your growth, and you chose to grow short in the shadows rather than rise above. When you did this, it had a profound mark on all those around you," Jesus said, beginning to feel the severe pain of the nails and his weight upon them.

"Jesus, would you like something to drink?" said one of the guards mockingly.

The guard dipped what looked like a rag into a shallow bowl and lifted it to Jesus on the end of his spear. Jesus tasted the wet cloth and scowled. The liquid was a bitter-tasting vinegar wine. The guard was playing a trick on him. Now Jesus, who was thirsty from the heat and the process of execution, was even thirstier and was to endure an agonizing set of moments. It was a cruel trick, but again Jesus forgave the man.

The man was cruel and without honor. Jesus returned his scorn with forgiveness and love. Billy again was filled with guilt. Each time in his life that he was challenged, he responded by blaming God rather than counting his blessings. He was reminded of a song that a local band sang at a bar back home. The song was called "Worse Than You" and was about how we all have it bad in this life. There are times when we lose hope and faith, but if we remember that someone else has it worse than you, we can draw strength and be strong together rather than blame fate or God.

The band handed out free albums at the show. The album sat in his car unopened for a long time before he looked down at it, as he sat for minutes during a long train passing at a railroad crossing. While he waited, he removed the plastic and put the album in. He skipped to the song he wanted to hear and played it. The song made him smile. It was a memorable tune with a good message.

He sang it to himself throughout the workday and as small challenges presented themselves at work or other places, he sang the chorus in his head. Realizing now the influence of a better mindset had been placed before him long before his journey here, he wondered why he did not pick up on its subtle intentions long ago rather than endure the last few years of challenges.

Billy also wondered why he did not remember the song as he saw paralytic people, John the Baptist, those possessed by demons, and others who had great challenges set before them. His good friend Balthazar reminded him to look outwardly at the blessings Billy already had rather than pity himself inwardly. He was not unique. His father passed away. He himself did not die. He allowed himself to grow small.

Jesus was right.

Balthazar was right.

Billy should have replaced his father as the large tree. The seed was planted correctly, but he chose to not grow properly. So many souls were affected by his stunted growth. His family and his community never had a taste of what his father offered after he passed because Billy never grew into the family man or community leader his father was before him. There was a bare spot in the forest because of his reluctance to offer himself as a servant.

Jesus was looking at Billy already when he said, "Your long journey is coming to an end. I am proud of you and know you have learned much from this journey. As with any change, you would have come to your own conclusions about how to live your life, but maybe not as quickly as with our help. Now you still have time to return and be the tree—the man you were supposed to be."

"I am truly grateful for what I have learned. I am humbled by those who have a more difficult lot in life and rise above it without much help from outside sources. If I die here on the cross, I will die knowing I could have done great things and have been a better man. If my actions were not so before in my time and place, they were so here, and my heart is content. I have regained my faith and blame no one for my father's death. It was time for the tree to fall in the forest. I did not replace him as I should, but here and now I am a better man and can die with dignity," said Billy.

"Your change is complete, Billy. Your heart and soul are righteous. But your time is not over here on this earth, only finished in this time and place. My Father works mysteriously. His plan is divine and greater than all of us. Just as I have a part to play in dying for the sins of humankind, you, too, still have a part to play in this world," said Jesus.

"I do not understand," said Billy as the weight of his body was evident in the pain he felt in his hands and feet.

"Save me as well," said the third criminal.

"Your heart is not like his," said Jesus. "Billy truly believes and wants nothing more than to do well in this world. You just want to avoid death without understanding what it means to be selfless or righteous," he continued.

No words could come from Billy as he looked at Jesus suffering. Billy prayed he could take the burden from Jesus and place it on himself. Billy had learned selflessness and saw the pain and torture Jesus was enduring. Although he was experiencing the same burden, he wanted to double his load and relieve the Son of God from his suffering.

"Let me take your pain from you, Jesus. Have your Father pour it on me. I will bear the sins. I will take your suffering from you," said Billy.

"Billy, you have become a good man and will grow to be an

even greater man. I must endure this experience myself. No one can take it from me," Jesus said, showing signs that his life was fading from him.

"I am sorry, Jesus. I feel useless. I will die, too, without helping you at all. I will die without growing into the tree I should have been," Billy said.

"Selfless to the end. Know this: My Father is expecting you. You will be with him eventually and me again as well, but not today. This day you will not join me in paradise, and you will not die. When you stepped into that shower so long ago and experienced coming here, it was because your physical body was struck. Your wife found you after she heard you fall. Your physical body was rushed for treatment. Your spiritual body was rushed here for treatment. Your physical body is in a hospital, unconscious, being attended to by physicians who think it is a miracle you are alive. Your spiritual body has been here with us. Now that you know your path and have become a better man with faith, your spiritual body will return and join your physical body."

With tears flowing down his face, mixing with the dry blood, Billy said to Jesus, "You and your Father are good to me. All of this has been very real for me, regardless of my physical body not being here."

Billy looked out from the cross one last time. He saw Balthazar, Eran, Anna, and the children. Balthazar slightly bowed his chin in reverence to Jesus and his friend. He had finally found Jesus as well. Eran and Anna wept, shielding their children's eyes from the gruesome scene.

Then Billy was drawn back as Jesus said, "Farewell, Billy. Close your eyes and witness the power of God."

CHAPTER 20

HOMECOMING

Comfortable and reclined, Billy woke up, unable to see or hear, just as before in the wilderness. He knew he was lying down. He could feel with his hands that he was on something comfortable, like a couch or a bed. He immediately discerned that he was not on a couch again, and he did so franticly. After years spent in Galilee, Jerusalem, and all parts of what Israel is now, on his feet working and trying to find Jesus, the last place he wanted to be was on a couch. From what he could tell, he was lying down on a narrow bed. His hands were encumbered with chords and wires. He sat up as best he could. Something was restraining his head from moving upward.

He remembered being in the wilderness and not having his sight and hearing for a brief time. It was frustrating and frightening. He took a deep breath and slowly exhaled out his nose. Having been through the loss of some senses before, he had faith they would gradually come back, and he would be able to assess his situation better and free himself from whatever was attached to him or holding him down.

He could feel his body and took an inventory of his hands and feet, realizing there was no sharp pain from the nails on the cross.

There was no aching pain in his neck and back from hanging on the cross. There was no pain to breathe in his chest and stomach.

When he was hanging on the cross next to Jesus, there was so much pain associated with the crucifixion. Speaking with Jesus after searching for him for so long compartmentalized his pain and allowed him to focus on Jesus's words, which acted as verbal relief to the painful execution. Billy was no longer on the cross.

Afraid to call out and with no knowledge of where he was, Billy whispered, "Jesus? Are you still here, Jesus?"

Jesus did not answer. Billy could hear machines above and behind him now. They were not noisy or clunky machines. They were steady, rhythmic machines, and they clearly sounded like something electric. Billy's hearing was the first of his two lost senses to come back. Now he had a small bit of light coming into his eyes, and he began to see very dull outlines. It was bright where he was; however, the illumination was not from the sun. Billy knew the sun after years spent in Israel. He knew the light as a source of warmth and heat as much as it was radiance.

There were so many times that he enjoyed and welcomed the warmth of the sun, and there were also several times in which the sun's warming properties were unbearable while on his journeys. Billy thought that the sun was a blessing from God, regardless of its more negative qualities. The light above him was electric. In addition to the hum of the machines next to him, the lights added a rhythmic dull pulse that filled the room.

As Billy lay listening intently, his eyes began to clear. Dull images now were becoming clearer. Colors starting with blue offered themselves to his vision instead of just the brightness of the lights. He was in a room. It was a room with very few ostentatious amenities. As his eyesight grew, he could see it was a sterile room.

The walls of the room were mostly white, but the wall facing him from where he lay was blue—the first color he was able to discover. He saw his feet move under white sheets and covers, and he recognized the metal rails along the sides and end of the narrow bed he was lying on. He was in a hospital. The hushed, metallic noises around him were machines monitoring his vital signs. Billy was no longer on the cross next to Jesus. He was back in his time in a hospital.

Jesus told him that he was struck down in the shower, and his physical body was taken to be healed. The situation was surreal. Billy now wondered if the entire experience was a dream. *How could it be*, Billy thought? Each moment was filled with rich senses and specific actions. If the experience were a dream, he had never had a dream of such magnitude and detail. No, there was no way what he had endured was a dream.

Starting with his immediate time on the cross, being an athlete when he was younger and getting injured, Billy knew pain, and the pain of the nails was real and intense. The crack of the whip of the head jailer—real. The taste of the blood from his head and face was real. The pain in his feet on the road to the crucifixion. The heat of the sun as he carried the cross and the warmth of the sun that brought comfort to his cold jail cell.

Then Billy contemplated the taste of the delicious grapes from the hidden vineyard and the experience of refreshment from the cool water of the natural spring. The intensity of the challenging push by the leopard and the snap of the snake. The intense feeling of fear from the demons was the only thing Billy experienced that seemed dreamlike, as if the conversations and interactions with their kind were isolated and remote, only to be experienced by Billy and Balthazar.

Finally, he concluded, the wine. He had never tasted such delicious wine. The wine was a delight blessed by the Son of God. Billy smiled and chuckled. He did not need proof of God's given experience for him, but of all the things that he did experience, the wine was what led him to his conclusion. He thought of Balthazar and knew he would think that amusing.

With his sight, hearing, and all other senses restored, Billy was able to feel that there was something on his head immobilizing him.

He reached up and felt around the top of his head at first. There were a lot of bandages. There was a strap of some kind on his chin as he lowered his hands across his face. It was difficult to remove the strap with the chords in his hands and arms, but he was able to do so. He then sat up and looked around the room. He removed the chords from his hand on his left hand first and then his right. Free from his mechanical and restrictive electrical prison, the machines made a different sound now.

They were angry machines, upset by Billy's actions, and they were calling out loudly, replacing the dull hum from before. Billy tried to sit up and felt a sharp pain throughout his head. The pain was intense, and he felt light-headed. He laid back down, which brought some comfort.

There was a door to the right of him that he had not paid attention to before it burst open. In charged a man in hospital scrubs. Billy noticed that the color of the scrubs were light blue, matching the wall that was in front of him. The man was clearly responding to the alarms of the machines. The man paused, with his mouth open and his eyes wide. Billy knew he was a surprise to the man.

The man stuttered, "You are awake. You are alive!"

Noticing the name tag on his badge at the end of a lanyard, Billy said, "Hello, John, my name is Billy."

John replied, "Yes. Yes, you are! Welcome back!"

"Where was I?" questioned Billy internally.

"You will not believe this, but you have been on life support and unconscious for some time. You were brought here after you suffered a—" the man could not finish, as more hospital staff poured into the room.

A woman wearing a long white coat, who had shoulder-length red hair and glasses, was the first to enter, and she rushed around to Billy's left side. She had a small flashlight in her hand and put one hand on Billy's forehead, gently shining it into his left and then right eye. The light was somewhat painful to Billy, as his eyes were still sensitive after the recovery of the sense.

"Billy, I don't know how to tell you this, but you should not be conscious. You should not be alive," said the woman, checking his pulse.

"He said I would witness the power of God," said Billy to the woman.

"I am Doctor Willington. I have been treating you. You have been through a lot. Brace yourself for what I am about to tell you. You suffered a brain aneurism in your home. You were rushed here to the hospital. You were unconscious when you arrived. Our staff quite honestly expected the worst outcome. It is unexpected that you pulled through. As a matter of fact, I should use the word *amazing* or *incredible* rather than *unexpected*."

"It is a miracle," said John.

"I do not like to use the word *miracle*. Everything that happens, happens for a reason. Divine intervention has little to do with a bulging brain artery and the survival of a patient," Dr. Willington said.

"I would strongly disagree, Doctor. But before this moment, the old me would have agreed with you. The old me would argue that God did not exist and did not influence the lives of those among us. But after my experience, I know that God influences us, our lives, and every living thing. He may not be the cause of all good, evil, love, hate, confidence, fear, and more, but I know what God can do and accomplish," said Billy.

"What are you saying?" asked the doctor.

"I am saying that right now I am here before you having experienced something dramatic and spiritual while I was gone. My soul or spirit was gone for years, and I met Jesus."

"Many people have spiritual experiences when they have trauma. It is simply your mind justifying the shock to your system. You did not meet Jesus; you think you met Jesus," said the doctor sternly.

"Doctor, I pray you are given the insight I have been blessed with to change your mind. How do you explain what has happened to me?" Billy said as he sat up and put his feet on the floor.

With the strength of a man who was filled with confidence, Billy took two steps toward the doctor, who backed up when Billy rose. His movement noticeably shocked her. Under the same circumstances, a normal patient would not be able to rise to his feet and walk. Billy showed no signs of impairment.

John said, "A miracle."

"Can one of you tell me where my wife and family are? I would very much like to see them," said Billy.

"Yes, yes. John, please let them know. I think they are still here in the building. We just met with them before the alerts on your life monitors and support systems were set off."

"Right away," said John as he rushed out the hospital room door.

"I meant what I said, Doctor. I realize you are a woman of science, and to you the spiritual world and the scientific world are separated by faith and facts, but I had an experience while my physical body was here. I hope you will come to understand that what has happened to me truly is a miracle influenced by God. If I am unable to convince you with words, maybe God will persuade you as he has done for me. As I told you, my faith was weak—no, it was nothing before now. I have changed because of what has happened. Maybe you, too, will have a newfound faith revealed to you as well."

As Billy finished his words, the doctor, with her hand on her mouth, seemed to be contemplating the physical and metaphysical situation before her. No words were shared between Dr. Willington and Billy. They stared at each other for a few seconds, and then the door opened. Billy's wife and children entered the room. The doctor's hand dropped away from her face, and she smiled to see the joyous reunion.

"May I ask that you lie or sit down, Billy? You have been through a lot, and I would prefer that you sit until we are able to run some tests to make sure everything is all right."

"Nonsense, I am never lying down again unless it is to sleep. I want to use every waking moment to love these people right here."

Mildred said, "How is this possible? The doctor told us you were not going to survive. The surgeries were unsuccessful. I am not complaining, but I want to understand how you are standing here before us when moments ago there was no hope."

"I can't explain what has happened. There is no medical explanation. This is a case that will need to be studied. But please, Billy, sit down. We must make sure you are all right," said the doctor.

Billy refused to sit down. He was given a second chance to be the father and husband he was meant to be. The family that was so far away from him while he chased after Jesus was in front of him, and he was going to show them the new person he had become through his experience. He took each family member separately into his arms and took a few moments to look at them deeply. Everyone was smiling. Everyone was filled with joy.

Billy convinced the doctor quickly that he was in full health. The doctor and hospital staff did their due diligence, making sure that he was clear to leave the hospital. Every test they ran was another positive step toward his freedom. He felt bottled up in the short time he was at the hospital and tried not to show his frustration as they poked at him. But in the end, it was well worth it to know he was 100 percent all right and safe to live the rest of his life. After all the tests, even the doctor was convinced his recovery was miraculous.

"I have never seen anything like this in my years as doctor. You are either very lucky or you have been touched by God's hand. Maybe both," said the doctor, keeping her head square but turning it to the side to show she was skeptical.

Billy's family took him home from the hospital. The doctor had set up several checkups to follow up, but he was given a bill of clean health. When they arrived at the house, they all walked in the front door. Billy's wife had made up a few sheets and set up a pillow on the couch for him. Billy's first action inside the house was to take the pillow, sheets, and blanket, fold them, and put them back in the side closet.

"Who wants to play a game," Billy said.

All three kids separately and loudly blurted out yes, and they agreed on Monopoly. Everyone sat down at the dinner table. They set up the game. and he looked around the table at everyone and released a deep breath. Billy was where he should have been the last several years, and he loved it. Deeply engaged in time with his family. His family. Not another family who took him in, though he enjoyed his time with them as well.

Later on that night, he made dinner for everyone. Not once did he touch the couch or think about turning on the television. Several friends and neighbors stopped by and brought food or just wanted to talk. Billy spoke to all of them eagerly, and they felt better having spoken to him.

A neighbor said, as Billy watched him walk down the steps of the porch, "I think that is the first time he has ever said more than five words to me, and he was looking me in the eye the entire time. He must have knocked something loose up there."

Billy smiled as he heard the man say those things. Being different from the man he was would be something all his friends and neighbors would notice. His family would grow stronger from his new attention. Each of the kids began to excel at their interests because he took a larger part in what they were doing. His wife found the dishes already done when she went to do them. She found the clothes washed, dried, and folded. The pets were fed and brushed.

He showed her love like never before by randomly buying her small gifts or flowers. He never went back to the couch. He enjoyed watching a ball game and some of the shows he used to watch, especially about large cats, but he always sat in a chair and never on the couch. He went to bed early and got up early. His wife also enjoyed the time with him in bed at the end of the day.

His work changed as well. His reviews were positive, and his coworkers grew to depend on him. His bosses did as well and showed their approval of his new attitude and effort by giving him consistent raises and promotions.

Billy reconnected with his old friend Steven. The first time they

met, Steven told the story of Lukie Lymen. Billy wept as he heard Steven tell the story. The two remained close friends until Steven passed away many years later.

In the community, he found himself coaching his kid's teams. Each team he coached admired him, and parents were glad to have him coach their children. He was involved in church and served on several local committees regarding organizations that mostly surrounded the children's interest.

Billy took time every morning and every night when he woke up and went to bed to say a prayer to God. He became more spiritual and meditated when time permitted. He did yoga three times a week and joined the YMCA, where he not only attended exercise courses but eventually taught some classes as well. His mind, body, and spirit were immersed in the moment and in helping others.

As he went to bed one night, with his wife next to him, listening, he said, "Dear Lord God, thank you for my family. Thank you for the time I have been allotted with them. Thank you for sending your son to this world to sacrifice for us. Forgive me for the sins I have committed that added to his torment on the cross. Thank you, Jesus, for giving yourself for all of us. Let us all learn from your service and sacrifice. And finally, thank you for second chances and new opportunities. May everyone who needs change find it through experience and help others who do not see their needs to find their best self. Thank you again and continue to bless my wife, children, and friends—from now and long ago—with happiness and health. May I be a part of their health and happiness until you finally call me home. Amen."